THE QUEST OF MALLORY BONES

THE QUEST OF MALLORY BONES

CODY FAVATA

Title: The Quest of Mallory Bones
Cover Artwork: Clara Bates
Cover and Interior Layout: Pickawoowoo Publishing Group
Edited: Eddie Elbrecht - Pickawoowoo Publishing Group
Printing & Distribution: Ingram (USA, UK, AUS, EUR)

ISBN: 978-1-7371070-0-2 (paperback)
ISBN: - 978-1-7371070-1-9 (hardback)
ISBN: - 978-1-7371070-2-6 (ebook)

First Printing, 2021

Chapter 1

A DEATH IN THE FAMILY

Rain pelted her bedroom window as she stared blankly out at the dark clouds that created a bitter, overcast sky. Her gazed dropped down to the wet cement that lay two stories below. A few puddles sat busy with ripples formed by the rain drops. The ripples were the Devil dancing in the rain because God was crying – this is something her mother always told her. Her mother… the thought made her freeze and her stare to become unfocused. Her mother had been missing for what seemed like an eternity. Time seemed to stand still as days dragged on and on. It had been two years and still nothing. No word, no clues as to her disappearance, she just seemed to vanish.

She leaned her head against the cool glass to try to subdue the headache that was beginning to swell. Her breath fogged up the glass and it reminded her of her own life – foggy and opaque. Just six months prior her father had been diagnosed with cancer. It began as stomach cancer and had since spread into his lymph nodes. Her mother's disappearance and her father's recent diagnosis were far too much to handle.

Her mother was a very confused woman. Before Mallory's birth she considered abortion. She wasn't ready to have a child, in fact she was angrier than a bat out of hell when she found out she was pregnant with her. She was a very angry woman who never seemed to be happy, even though her father tried his very best to give her everything she wanted. Morgana Frost grew up in a very broken home, which, unfortunately, got the better part of her and broke it in half. Somewhere along the path of life she buried her decency under a pile of stone and ice and grew up with only a fraction of what was once a happy, little girl.

Her father also grew up in a broken home; however, he took a different path in life and was able to retain a rather humble demeanor. He was a very pleasant man who always tried his best to keep a genuine smile on his face. Michael Bones was a very generous man who kept his head held high.

He entered the room with a slight cough which unnerved Mallory even more. She knew of his diagnosis and understood the severity of it. She wished every day she could cure him. She choked back the tears that lined her lower eyelids.

"Mallory, honey, how are you holding up?"

She swallowed hard as a white lie escaped her tight lips. "I'm fine. I'll be alright." She forced a smile that her father knew all too well to be false.

"The burial begins in an hour. We should get going soon." The last of these words were choked out which caused Mallory to flinch again.

"Let me just grab my coat." She walked over to her wooden desk chair and grabbed her black, wool coat that was carelessly draped over the backrest. Her blonde hair fluttered effortlessly down the back of the coat as she fastened the buttons all the way up to her neck. She wore a black dress underneath and some black shoes to match. Her blue eyes and blonde hair were a stark contrast to the darkness that covered her – like a ray of hope during the darkest of times.

She followed her father out of the room and down the stairs to the front door. Before they left she took one last look back at the fireplace on which sat a picture of her family – her mother, her father, and herself just a few years younger – inside that very home and near that very same fireplace. She turned around and both left without another word.

The hearse sat silent under the big oak tree parked just a few feet away from the spot reserved for her mother's coffin. The coffin, of course, was empty. The body of her mother was never found, but after two years with no trace the police declared her as deceased. The pallbearers who carried the empty casket kept stoic faces of silence and sadness. Michael's parents were already dead and only Morgana's father remained alive. He stood next to Michael and Mallory in silence out of respect for not only his daughter but also for the man that his daughter loved like no other.

The wake, held just a week prior, was small and only those close to the family attended. The minister of the burial service said his prayers while mostly everyone sat in silence with the occasional whimper or moan escaping from the crowd that attended. Michael grabbed Mallory's hand and a small stream of tears fell from both of their eyes. They let their tears flow as if to let all the sadness leave their body, not wanting it to return, but with Michael's sickness it was only a matter of time. Mallory carried a single sunflower, her favorite, which she placed on her mother's casket as it was lowered into the grave. A small handful of dirt was thrown on top. From earth you come and to which you return.

At the reception everyone approached Michael and Mallory with careful ease submitting their condolences and praising both for being strong during such a difficult time. They thanked everyone for coming and the service ended as modestly and as comfortably as possible. Father and daughter headed home, both with completely different thoughts on their minds. Mallory, sitting in silence, promised herself at that moment she would do whatever it took to find a cure for her father.

Chapter 2

A MOST PECULIAR BOOK

Concept of a story isn't always what it seems.
Sometimes even empty books are filled with hopes and dreams.
The pages fill with tales of mind and those of noble heart.
Even from fantastic worlds and surreal lands apart.

Her hand gripped the handle to the door of the old bookstore that sat on the corner of Maple and Elm Streets. Like most towns, Meyersville used tree names for its innermost streets. Like most towns' bookstores, Meyersville's was old and mostly made of brick, some so old it felt like they could and would crumble over your head. *A Darn Good Read* was this type of old, but Mallory summoned up the courage to venture on inside. She loved to read which is why she found it so odd that she had never been into this bookstore before. She had visited her local library countless times. It was as if she'd never seen this place, yet here she was standing amidst a sea of books. She casually paced up and down the aisles to get a feel for which types of books were located where and how that specific shop laid out its Dewey Decimal System. After a brief tour she made her way to the desk that sat between the seemingly endless shelves of stories. There, in a chair that faced away from her, sat an elderly man. The back of his balding head peeked over the top of the brown, leather chair.

"Excuse me," Mallory's voice held a slight quiver. The man in the chair sat upright from his relaxed position and turned around; his remaining hair salt and peppered and his face stoic. A pipe tilted out of the right corner of his mouth.

"Ahh," he stood up and walked to the edge of the desk. He took the pipe out of his mouth to speak. "It's not often I see youth in here. What can I do for you," he finished as he returned the pipe to his mouth, his voice a little rough.

Mallory kept a confident tone in her voice. "I'm just wondering what you might recommend for…"

"Well, what is your reading level," the elderly man interrupted in a gruff voice.

"Sublime, thank you!" Her response came a bit angry, but she felt it called for after being interrupted. She swore she could see the man let out a quick, sly smile.

He allowed for a short pause this time before asking, "What is your name, miss?"

"Mallory," she responded. "Mallory Bones."

"Bones?" the man questioned. "That's a very unusual last name."

"I get that often," she replied.

"So you're looking for a book, but what kind of book?"

"I'm trying to escape," she paused, "mentally," she finished.

"Hmm," the old man squinted at her. "Follow me," he gestured with his pipe. She followed him through a jungle of aisles and books. As she passed by she noticed some familiar titles such as *The Old Man and the Sea*, *The Great Gatsby* and *Cujo*, along with some less familiar titles such as *Autumn Knight and the Whispering Willows* and other books that seemed to follow in a series. Eventually, the man settled on a specific spot which played host to one of the best adventure books of all time, *The Adventures of Huckleberry Finn*. On the top shelf, which was a shelf up and a few books over, hidden between a few thick books, sat an old, dusty one.

"Hey," Mallory said softly, "what's this?" She pulled the book out. The book didn't have a title, or an author. In fact, it was simply a black, hardcover book with only a strange symbol on it made out of a light metal. The symbol was a circle with an "M" the stretch of its diameter and a "T" that filled it the opposite way.

"Don't worry about that book," the old man said. His stare was directly into her eyes, but something seemed a little off as he let out a small smile.

"But… why not? It doesn't even have a title?" She peeled it open quickly and rapidly flipped the pages. To her surprise, all of them were blank. She had a questioning look on her face. She was confused and concerned at the same time. "What kind of a book doesn't have words?"

"Why don't you take it home then?" the old man queried smiling. "Read it."

"But…" she started before he broke in again.

"Take it. Keep it," he urged before finally adding, "Books aren't always what they seem. Before you do that let me just go take care of some paperwork real quick. May I see it please?"

"Really?" Mallory beamed. "I can keep it?"

"If you can handle it, it's yours," he said. Mallory handed the book over. "Come get this in about three minutes. The paperwork won't take long. While you wait, take a look around and see what else you want." He smiled once more before leaving the aisle and working his way back to the desk.

After he was out of sight she took up his offer and looked at a few more books. She found one she thought might be interesting titled *The Lands of Forgotten Time*. She read the back and held it against her chest and made her way back over to the desk only to find that the man had seemingly disappeared. The untitled book sat alone on his desk. She placed her book down beside it.

"Hello?" she asked as she looked around. She looked everywhere for him and realized he wasn't anywhere to be found inside the bookstore. "Well, he did say I could keep it." After the brief personal communication she picked up the books from the table but realized she hadn't paid for the other. She put it down and figured she could always come back for it, except she didn't know how long it would be before she visited again. She left the store without looking back.

When she arrived at home she went directly to her room. After getting comfortable in her reading chair, she noticed that the symbol could be detached from the book. She peeled it off and set it aside then opened the book itself. The first few pages were blank. She closed the book with a horrible feeling that she had been tricked. She peered over at the clock on her desk which lit up with numbers symbolizing that it was 2 p.m. She took the symbol in her hand and looked at it again. Nothing seemed wrong or strange until she decided to open the book while holding onto the symbol. She flipped the cover over to open the book and a blinding flash of white light surrounded her. When she came to, her vision was back to normal and she couldn't believe her eyes.

Chapter 3

A NEW WORLD

A new start in a strange land,
Like nothing you've ever seen.
Create a new sense of adventure,
Begin anew;
Let the past erode and ween.

Blurry vision suddenly gave way to an unmistakably clear, yet confusing observation. No longer was Mallory sitting at her desk but in a forest surrounded by huge evergreen trees which seemed full and healthy. Adjacent to her was a stone pillar which came to a point at the top in a pyramid shape. Sitting atop the apex was the same symbol as the one she took off the book. She looked around questioningly before looking down at her hand. Wrapped inside her curled fingers was the symbol. It was still with her. She closed her eyes and took in a deep breath. She was dreaming; she had to be. That's just it she thought to herself – she had fallen asleep and was now dreaming. She tried a variety of small gestures such as shaking her head to try to wake up. Nothing was working and she began to panic.

"Okay," she muttered to herself. "Maybe if I pinch myself I'll wake up." She did as she instructed and nothing happened. She squinted briefly at the pain from the pinch. "This calls for drastic measures," she continued and then proceeded to punch herself in the gut. The pain was rough but still nothing. "This is one hell of a dream," she exclaimed. She looked down to make sure her whole body was with her and that nothing was amiss. As she was looking down at her feet a voice called out.

"Hello?" The voice was deep, unmistakably male. It startled Mallory as she looked up and clutched the symbol to her chest. A man appeared from behind a pair of what seemed to be raspberry bushes. "Who are you?" the voice had a strange accent but seemed English in origin, which just confused her even more.

Mallory was hesitant to answer at first. It seemed odd to talk to a stranger; especially in what she still believed was a dream. However, being a dream it couldn't hurt right? She'd just wake up. "My name is Mallory, Mallory Bones."

As the man came more into focus she noticed he was a bit taller, around six foot three inches tall. He had long brown hair that was braided down his back but his most distinguishable trait besides his royal purple eyes was his ears. They were close to his head but jutted out the back and came to a point at their ends.

"Mallory Bones, my name is Lee. I come from a village not too far from here. Where do you hail from?" His gaze focused on her as if trying to decipher ancient runes.

"This has got to be a dream," she replied as she looked the man up and down.

"Dream," he responded. "I'm not sure I understand. Here," he took her hand. "See, I am real. This forest is real and this place is very sacred. How are you aware of its location?"

"But," she started, "I was in my room, I was going to read that book. I took this symbol off…"

"What book?" he cut in and his voice was full of question yet somehow understanding.

"The black book on my desk. It had blank pages inside it and this on the cover." She extended her hand and opened her palm to expose the symbol.

"Where did you get that?" His voice suddenly became stern and his gaze sharpened. He didn't take his eyes off hers.

"It came off the book I was given at the bookstore. The man said I could keep it. I brought it home and…" She came back to the reality that she was not in the comfort of her own home, or her own room. "Where am I?" she asked.

"This is the forest of Algernon. This world is called Everworld," Lee responded.

"Everworld? What is Everworld?"

Lee squinted at her. "Are you from another world? Are you from the world called Earth? The place that stories call Earth?"

"Yes, isn't this Earth?" Mallory questioned.

"Earth is a place that's only in stories in our land." Lee responded. "This is Everworld," he repeated.

"I have to be dreaming," she repeated.

"I can assure you that you're not."

A look of confusion contorted with that of anger. Frustration began to set in. Her eyes darkened. She almost wept.

Somehow sensing the oncoming outburst Lee said, "Why don't you follow me back to my village. More can be explained there by our queen. Your looks give it away that you're not from here. I'll have you speak to Queen Evana. She and the other villagers will understand."

"Am I the only human of this world?" Mallory asked.

"No," Lee countered. "For example, I am elvish," he explained, "and the center city in the middle of Everworld is home to the Humanus. They may have your physical structure but they don't have your hair color. There is no other person in this entire world who possesses the hair color of straw."

"Follow me, Mallory Bones, there is a path not too far from this sacred structure that leads back to my home."

"Alright," she agreed. She didn't really have a choice did she? She had come to a strange land and met an elf. She still wasn't fully convinced this wasn't a dream either and proceeded to follow him to a path not too far from where they were. Every ounce of her being wished she would just wake up, but this wasn't a dream. Everything seemed all too real, felt too real and smelled too real.

The path they walked on was made of dirt. She had to pick up her own pace to keep up with that of Lee's. She fell behind periodically. She noticed strapped to his back were two separate weapons. One was a quiver which held beautiful arrows that appeared hand-crafted. The quiver was gold and had white details down the side with some elvish print down its front. The other was a sword, which also seemed to have been forged by the hand of a master metalsmith. Its sheath was also beautiful and was of the same color scheme and distinction. His garments consisted of green robes, belts and a cloak with a shawl. His boots were black and mid-calf high.

She looked back down at her own clothes. She was wearing the same thing she remembered wearing while last being at home. She picked up her pace and caught up to him.

"Lee, how do I get back home?" Mallory's voice was full of uncertainty.

"I'm not sure," Lee responded but his pace didn't slow. "That's something to ask Queen Evana. She'll know more about this situation than I do. I'm simply a warrior of the Elven Tribes. That's why I was out in the woods. I was training before I heard you."

The rest of the walk was mostly quiet. Mallory put the symbol clutched in her hand back into her pocket. Her eyes skirted the woods they passed and for the first time realized how sweet the air smelled. It was clean of pathogens and other toxins, something very unfamiliar to her. The trees were a green that seemed more vibrant and the sky a dark blue that matched the intensity of Lee's eyes. Everything seemed calm. She heard a rustle off in the distance and looked over in its direction to find a creature she'd never seen before scurry about the beautiful and thick woods. The woods didn't even appear to be darkened by the massive amount of forest that shaded this part of Everworld.

"If you are from Earth, you'll see many creatures here that you may not recognize. If the stories are true then our world is very different from your own. Try not to get too excited for it may cause a stir and create panic within our realm. We've been at peace here for the last thirty years, but lately troubles have started occurring. But enough of that for now, we must get you to Algernon."

They continued for some time along the dirt path until a clearing came into view. Groves of homes were crafted into the giant trees that surrounded the small opening, and sitting in the middle of the opening was a fountain made of stone.

Chapter 4

CASTLE OF SHADOWS; QUEEN OF DARKNESS

Shadows are the home of darkness.
The closer it gets to light, the bigger a shadow becomes.
The light can burn the dark away,
If only for a moment to save;
The dark from which the light was born.

Upon a throne of black-coated steel and decorated with gems of amethyst and rubies sat a woman whose eyes could cause even the most noble of blue-blooded individuals to return to a commonwealth status. Her eyes were as yellow as topaz and her hair as dark as the night itself. Raven-like, her black hair was cut short in the back and grew longer as her bangs fell to her chin. Her cold, yellow eyes lay stoic inside the sockets of smooth white skin that covered the face of the evil queen, most unlike the rough skin of the boar-like creatures that guarded her and her palace. Her bright, intense eyes were a contradiction of her heart that was as cold as the ice that carves the winds of a northern winter's night. Her facial features were sharp and her nose came to a dull point. Placed upon her head was a crown made of crystals that shimmered in the moonlight that snuck into the castle in the dead of the night.

To her left and right were two guards that kept watch over her. They weren't of human origin. Their faces were that of boars, and thick tusks protruded from the corners of their mouths. Beady eyes sat in sunken sockets which were placed just about short snouts. Heavy, metal helmets covered their heads helping to build more muscles on their already broad shoulders and a thick skin covered their muscular bodies. They had human-like hands and feet, seemingly built to be warriors. The Centrions were of the Boar Kingdoms that resided in the Muddy Hills region of Everworld.

"My queen," a deep voice came from a larger Centrion entering the queen's chamber. The queen draped her arms along the chair and rested her hands along its edge as her fingers curled around the end of the arm rests. The Centrion stopped about ten paces from the throne.

"You bring me news, Krum?" The queen's demeanor didn't change.

"Yes, my queen. Our army has increased two-fold over the last five years. They should be fully prepared within the next few weeks to attack on your command. The entirety of Everworld shall be yours." He dropped to a knee and bowed his head.

A small, clear orb sat on a red, velvet pillow which lay open on the Dark Queen's lap. Dark clouds formed inside the ball. She closed her eyes and let out a deep sigh of relief before looking down. Moonlight shimmered off the crystal of the orb and she peered into it; an image began to appear. The image suddenly became blurry. Something was preventing the picture from forming clearly. She squinted her eyes. This situation had never taken place. The images that formed inside her crystal orb had always been clear and concise. This image seemed to drag on, like it was holding on to something.

"My queen?" Krum questioned. His brow furrowed as he looked in distress at the queen whose face was now almost contorted with frustration.

"It's nothing," she replied rather quickly and set the crystal and pillow aside on a table top that sat right next to her throne. She had always commanded with a strong voice. Her ascendance to the throne followed the death of the evil sorceress, Evelyn, who helped her come to understand this new strange land. She was not from Everworld. She too came from Earth. Evelyn found her lost and confused in the very woods near the same ruins where Mallory was found. After Evelyn found her she brought her back to the Castle of Shadows where she proceeded to help educate her in the ways of Everworld.

The Castle of Shadows was enormous. It was made of beautiful, black granite and covered a large portion of land. Most of the castle was uninhabited and lay cold and barren. The prisoners who once helped take care of the castle died along with the sorceress and her curse. The castle was once bright and beautiful. It was called Westershire, as it lay in the western most realms of Everworld. It was once the most beautiful castle in the entirety of Everworld. The sorceress used to be of noble and good heart before she lost it after a wizard named Azaroth broke her heart. Azaroth was a selfish wizard from the most southern realms of Everworld in Undershire. After the series of events occurred that caused him to break her heart she became cold and eventually found the village and castle of Westershire which she claimed as her own. Using her powers she quickly took control of the castle and all its inhabitants after killing off the king and queen. Her heart became stone and the evil began to ooze out of her every pore like black beads of sweat. After control had been taken and the palace secured she cursed the entire village. The village became a deserted wasteland and everyone was forced to work at the castle. Anyone caught trying to escape was instantly killed. The prisoners lived in fear. The only way to break the curse was if the evil queen could find good in her own heart and good in someone she loved. Alas, the years dragged on like dense sand falling through a bottleneck hourglass. She couldn't find another love, for her heart always belonged to Azaroth.

Azaroth had a twin, Azarim. Unlike Azaroth, Azarim was the yin to Azaroth's yang. If Evelyn could have met Azarim it's almost certain she would have fallen for him and the curse would have been lifted, but Azaroth never spoke of Evelyn and Azarim never found out.

Krum noticed the queen's uneasiness and spoke cautiously. "Queen A…" started Krum before he was sharply cut off.

"Do not speak my name, for I fear there is more in store than what we think. My time with Evelyn before her untimely death taught me much, and one of them was a sixth sense for bad situations. Something feels off. Something feels…" she paused and clutched a choker necklace that hung around her neck. The necklace was sterling silver, and a silver letter "M" hung from it. "…different," she finished, as Krum snorted in disgust at the unwelcome news.

Chapter 5

VILLAGE OF ALGERNON; QUEEN EVANA

A hundred years by, the princess stands
With rule over the Elven Lands
For she knows not what's at stake
A war soon lies in future's wake

A beautiful Elven woman sat upon a fountain of hand-carved stone that lay in the clearing of Algernon; that woman was none other than Queen Evana. Her age was astounding, even though her appearance showed her years to be no more than that of a young adult just coming out of her teens. She dressed in the most beautiful garments, purple and sky blue in color, clearly hand-woven from the finest tailors of Algernon, and put together with great pride and delicacy. Surrounding the curve of her brow and forehead was a headdress ring of gold. It curved up to a point in the middle of her forehead and wrapped just so perfectly around the back where it sat over a perfect large braid that traveled down the length of her slender back.

Lee walked slowly with Mallory over to where the queen sat. He dropped to a knee motioning Mallory to do the same.

"Queen Evana," he began with his head bowed and raised it to look into her eyes, a sign of respect.

"Lee, welcome back from your trip." She turned to face Mallory. "Hello, young one. I am Queen Evana." Mallory stood frozen. Queen Evana's voice was soft, almost nurturing, like that of a mother caring for a sick child. "Who might you be?"

Mallory unfroze from her shocked stance and bowed. "Queen Evana, my name is Mallory."

"Mallory, what is your family name?"

"Bones," Mallory responded. She believed she saw a glint of something that resembled hope in the queen's eyes.

"Mallory Bones, welcome to Algernon. I can tell you are not from this world. The color gives it away." Evana paused for a brief second then added, "You seem somewhat familiar to me. I know this may seem impossible, but it's like I've met you before."

Mallory stood staring into the queen's eyes. She blinked and looked away realizing how rude she appeared. Then, something hit her that had seemed to keep itself locked away in the shock of her being in this new world. Her father was sick, and probably worried sick too.

"I don't have an answer for you, Queen Evana. I'm sorry to say but I've never met you before in my life. I come from a place called Earth. My father is sick, very, very sick with a deadly disease called cancer. I must return to Earth."

"Cancer?" the queen's voice was full of question "What is cancer?" The word rolled off her tongue leaving a disgusting taste in her mouth and she was unsure why until Mallory explained it to her.

"We have something very similar to that here in Everworld. We call it, 'the Final Death'."

"Seems about right," Mallory retorted. "I must get back. My mother ran away when I was very young. My father is all I have left and I am all that he has left." Her eyes dropped and tears filled them to the brim, but didn't spill over.

Queen Evana pulled Mallory down close to her on the stone fountain. She hugged her tight and the tears seemed to disappear from her eyes. Warmth came over her like everything was going to be alright. Mallory looked over at the center of the fountain. Two initials were structured into the middle stone of the fountain itself along with a small sentence, it read: *This fountain is dedicated to the man that saved us all from the wrath of The Darkness; MB.* Those were the same initials she had. She found it to be a very odd coincidence then quickly turned her attention back to Evana.

"Mallory, there is hope for your father yet. In the north of Everworld lies a spring with water that holds the power to heal any and all sickness. We do not draw from this spring unless it's to cure the most deadly of diseases or wounds. Supply of this water is low and we must make sure it has time to refill itself before it runs dry from overuse."

"Could I..." she couldn't find it in herself to form the full sentence.

"You can. Tonight after you get settled I'll have Lee stop by where you will be staying and drop you off a vial necklace you can fill from the spring. Be forewarned, the journey to the spring is not easy and comes at great risks. But sometimes to fix peril, you must take a big risk yourself." Evana stood up from her seated position. "Now, if you will, please follow me to your temporary dwelling."

"But, how do I get back?"

"That will be explained in time, I promise, but first I must tell you a story." As they walked toward Mallory's temporary dwelling Evana told Mallory the tale of the recent war which ravaged the entirety of Everworld just a few decades earlier.

Thirty years ago there was a terrible uprising. An evil wizard named Azaroth sought to take control of all of Everworld with the help of a Sorceress named Evelyn Severa. Evelyn was once a very good sorceress; she used her powers for nothing more than to help those in need. Her lineage dates back thousands of years and her family was known for helping others and keeping peace within the realms of Everworld. Azaroth had gotten word of a beautiful sorceress who had come into womanhood in a village called Pendlesham near the eastern border of the western city of Westershire. Her father had already been dead for some time. Azaroth wanted power and he knew that with his charm and the help of a little magic he could woo her into falling in love with him. Azaroth visited Pendlesham and demanded a meeting with the sorceress. Almost all inhabitants of Everworld knew of Azaroth and his powers, so nobody fought against this command including Evelyn's mother. Her mother was old and not strong enough anymore to stand up to Azaroth. Azaroth beckoned Evelyn to have a meal with him and she obliged fearing the worst for the people of Pendlesham which her family swore to protect. During that dinner, Azaroth slipped an odorless, strong love potion into her drink and shortly after that first encounter she began to fall for him. He played the part, delivering charm and an infectious smile courtesy of his magic. How could she turn down a man who seemed so charming despite the stories? After all, they were just stories, tales of old. After a few years Evelyn became the bride of Azaroth and Pendlesham became his kingdom. Around this time Azaroth's brother Azarim got word of his brother's marriage and knew instantly what Azaroth's true intentions were.

One fall night when the moon was full and the air was still warm with the final traces of summer, Azaroth took Evelyn's hand and told her what he envisioned for himself and his beautiful bride – the whole of Everworld to be theirs. Evelyn, originally pure of heart, denied this quite possible opportunity. Azaroth pleaded with her, begged her, but her heart disagreed and she refused to take part in his quest for power. The man she had thought was incredibly charming and nothing like the stories of old turned out to be the same monster portrayed in the tales. Azaroth turned on Evelyn, killing her mother one night while she slept and some of the men of Pendlesham. He left her and Evelyn's heart broke into fragments. It was now atoms of what used to be a beautiful soul. Her once warm eyes turned cold and her soul became dark. She became stronger and fiercer. She lost control of her prior self and the once brave and beautiful sorceress was now an evil, disgusting being full of hate and misery. Wrapped up in her own grief she left Pendlesham, breaking her family's promise to protect them and headed west toward Westershire. What happened to Westershire is described as nothing short of a massacre. Evelyn took control of the castle and killed king Destin and his queen, Lizabeth. Westershire was now under her command. However, she didn't stop there. She made it her quest to kill Azaroth. She amassed an army of Centrions who lived in the Muddy Hills region that adjoined the western border of Westershire. With the help of the Centrions war broke out and the first great war of Everworld began. While

Evelyn amassed her armies in Westershire, in Northern Town in the northernmost parts of Everworld, Azarim confronted Azaroth and promised to punish him for his unethical and devilish ways, but Azaroth evaded capture and disappeared. He hasn't been heard from since.

While war raged on for twenty years and ravaged the land, a young man from Earth showed up in Everworld. Azarim was the first to find this young man who was around the age of sixteen. The young man trained under the old wizard and fought on the side of good. His goal wasn't to ultimately kill Evelyn but to mend her heart so the war could be over. Azarim brought him to me, where he also trained with our most skilled warriors. Other nations fought alongside us in the war for many years. After five years of fighting, he finally came face to face with Evelyn, where he was able to mend a little of the evil sorceress's heart but he couldn't fully mend it. He convinced her to stop the fighting. She was still heartbroken and unforgiving but he promised her that if she stopped the war he would let her live. Evelyn agreed and the war ended. After a brief stay in a peaceful Everworld he returned to Earth. That young man is a hero in this world. His name...was Michael Bones.

Mallory's eyes widened and her throat closed up. Her tongue seemed to swell in the back of her throat and her head began to swim. They had reached Mallory's temporary dwelling and she nearly fainted onto the bed supplied for her.

"That's..." she paused, gasping for air. "That's my fa..." she tried again but couldn't finish.

Evana placed a hand on her shoulder. "That's your father's name isn't it? I knew you looked familiar, you have his eyes." She sat on the bed that Mallory had almost passed out onto. "I can only imagine how hard and unbelievable this must be to hear, but it's all true, written down in our very own history books."

Mallory couldn't bear to look up. Her head swam in a raging river that seemed to flow through the brome of her being and leak out of all the ducts and crooks of her eyes and nose.

"Take some time to let this settle in. I shall leave you in peace until tomorrow morning when you start your journey. Until the moon is high, Lee will stand guard over you and shall you need him or I do not hesitate to ask. It's only acceptable and rather obvious that you may have questions."

Evana left leaving Mallory and Lee, but Mallory remained mostly silent and just thought. She thought better in silence, things always sounded better in her head anyways. Instead of asking Lee about the war she asked him more about Algernon and about Everworld and what she might encounter on their journey. He told her to get some sleep. The moon was high in the sky and she would need rest noting that traveling in an unfamiliar world would be stress enough on the body let alone the physicality involved. He wished her a restful sleep and closed the door behind him. She looked out a window and watched Lee walk toward his own home, watching the man who be her insight into a world that had more in store for her than she could ever dream.

An empty bag sat nestled along the edge of her round dwelling. This bag would be filled with necessary supplies, but also with the hopes and dreams of a young girl lost and confused in a big new world. Tomorrow this bag would be half full, only to be filled along the way as her journey reached its end.

Mallory changed into a night gown that was given to her earlier by an elvish maid while she talked to Lee. She lay down and closed her eyes. Visions of war flashed in her head like explosions. Thoughts

of lines of men crashing into each other with rivers of blood taint-
ing the streams she's so far seen in this world a rosé pink. She shook
them best as she could from her mind's eye, turned on her side and
fell asleep to the silence that surrounded her in the beautiful village
of Algernon.

Chapter 6

LIKE FATHER LIKE DAUGHTER

Every path you choose, every chance you take
Every road leads to, every risk you make.
Like father like son, like mother like daughter
Like father like daughter, like mother like son
It calls you.

A large clock decorated with thick, black roman numerals hung on the wall in the living room right above the fireplace. The soft glow of the fire poured out into the serene room that seemed to grow ever louder the quieter it got. Michael lounged in a recliner that was backlit by a standing lamp that occupied a corner of the room. Pressed to his face was a hardcover book titled *Quiet in the Kill of Night*. The rhythmic tick-tock of the clock was drowned out by the crackle of the fire. A rather large pocket of moisture came into contact with the heat of the blaze and created a rather loud pop. The ashes that followed fluttered down and out onto the bricks that lined the fireplace; it caught his attention enough to cause him to mark his position along the journey of his book. He grabbed the broom and dustpan meant for the fire and swept the ashes into it and poured them back in. Michael placed the dustpan and broom down and arched his back in a big stretch that he hoped would relieve the kinks that seemed to be forming. He had been sitting a while and figured this would be as good a time as any to take a break.

The air seemed too stagnant, too quiet. He left the comfort of the living room of his own to see how his daughter was doing. These last months, let alone days – with the burial and all – hadn't been the easiest and he knew how essential this time was. He was careful not to spend too much time with Mallory, as he knew she would need time for herself to think things through – she was just like him in that sense – but he also knew it was important he be there for her, with her. After climbing the stairs to her room to find her door shut tight, he rapped lightly on the frame and waited patiently for a reply. When no reply came he tried again, a little louder, but, alas, the same response ensued. It wasn't like her to ignore him so he figured she must be asleep. He cracked the door open just enough to see how she was doing, sleeping or not, but to his surprise she was nowhere to be seen and it was unlike her to leave the house without telling him where she was going, especially this late at night.

He entered her room and noticed her scarf draped lazily over the backrest of her chair. To him it seemed she couldn't have gone far… or…could she have? As he walked over to her desk he noticed a book opened and printed on the pages were scattered words. He blinked his eyes a few times to make sure what he was seeing was proper. How could it be that she had a partially completed book at her disposal? After reading a few of the misplaced words, one in particular stuck out at him: "Mallory…" He immediately closed the book to read the cover but soon came to discover the same problem Mallory faced when she attempted to read it; there was no title or author, just an empty space where the symbol used to be before Mallory took it off. Michael, again, flipped the first page open, except words came. Words began forming in front of his eyes. He rubbed his eyes and looked down again as more words began to form. The book now had his attention. He read along as more words came into being: *Algernon was to be where it all began. Mallory and* – and there it was again. Mallory's name appeared in this book. Obviously Mallory was not the only Mallory in existence but what was the pure luck of his daughter acquiring a book with a main character who shared the same first name? He read on until the words ended: *…and Lee would set off at daybreak in search for her father's cure…* Michael couldn't help but smile at this. He knew his daughter's passion and if Mallory thought she could find a way to save him, she would do it no matter what the cost.

Michael didn't yet realize just how close this book would hit to home. He read on: *Little did Mallory know just how much things had changed since her father's last visit during the war. Never having been here before she never needed to.* Michael was forced to squint his eyes and re-read that last line again. He flipped the cover back over, studied it again – it was still blank. He flipped the book back open to its mark and read on: *Algernon still…*

"No!" Michael said slowly as his hands began to tremble. He gently laid the book down on its face as the pages and words flipped open in a mocking frenzy.

Words began to surface on the pages that confirmed his greatest fear, yet a most improbable predicament…*Algernon still had its secrets.* Michael looked down in horror as the pages slowly filled with words confirming the impossibilities of what appeared in front of his eyes.

"Mallory, please, no!" Michael boomed into the open book, but try as hard as he might, his acoustics couldn't penetrate the boundaries that lay just past the grasp of reality and fiction. He knew exactly how to get back into the literary work to save her, but he didn't know what good it would do with him in his current state. All he could do now was read on in hopes his daughter had the same fortitude he carried when he was younger. He settled down on Mallory's bed with the book and read along as her story now took its turn unfolding in the pages of Everworld. He followed along until the words halted with her falling asleep peacefully in the little town of Algernon, and he fell asleep as she did, hoping to wake before her.

Chapter 7

ON YOUR MARK, GET SET, GO!

Paint the rose a subtle red
Shade the sky to grays
New clouds forming left for dead
New light shines on her like rays
'Till you're beckoned by the moon
Ghosts will sweep the clouds at night
Drift afloat by starlight's noon
Hear them calling white and bright

Rectangular rays of sunshine spilled over the window ledges inside the temporary dwelling that Mallory slept quietly in. A knock rattled the wooden door waking her from a particularly confusing dream. She sat up slowly and yawned, stretched her arms over her head and proceeded to stand up. She walked clumsily over to the door slowly regaining her balance and opened it to find Lee standing there wearing garb similar to what he wore yesterday except the colors had been changed from greens to whites with green accents.

"Good morning, Mallory," Lee said as he proceeded to enter her room. He looked over at the unmade bed and shook his head.

Mallory took notice. "Well, Lee, what were you expecting? Your knock woke me up. All I've had time to do is answer the door."

"You sleep late," Lee replied.

"Late?" Mallory questioned. "What time is it?"

"The sun is already high in the sky. It's just before midday." Lee's response came swiftly as he walked over to the empty bag along the wall which he picked up and brought to Mallory. "Fill this with essentials. Our journey is a long one. Don't take too much or you'll regret it. The weight will begin to become too much."

Mallory quickly filled the bag with clothing that had been neatly laid out during the night and strapped a canteen along the side that she would fill with water from the fountain before they set off. All Lee had strapped to him was his bow and a quiver full of handmade arrows.

"Is that all you plan to bring?" she asked Lee.

"Aye," came his retort, "'Tis all I need." He flashed a canteen also strapped to his side. "Fix yourself for the day and let's be off. I know how badly you must want to retrieve the purest water from the Silver Lake."

"The Silver Lake?" Mallory asked.

"Yes," Lee answered. "That's the name of the spring in the far north that holds the water that can cure all sicknesses. Its domain is protected by an ancient family of powerful fairies. Queen Evana will give you a vile with a very special engraving. When we show this engraving to the ruler of their domain we will be allowed one and only one vile full of water. They will be with us while we retrieve it to make sure we only take our allowance."

"These fairies," Mallory questioned, "are they kind?"

"They are kind, but they are also very powerful, and any thought or chance to provoke them will create dire consequences," Lee warned as his eyes narrowed.

"Am I allowed to get dressed in private?" Mallory's sarcasm didn't exactly strike Lee as she had hoped.

"Alright, but hurry, we must waste no more time," Lee answered quickly. "I expect you to take no more than five minutes." He left her to change. She donned the same clothes as the day before – a black shirt with a jack-o-lantern on it, an orange and black flannel, gray skinny jeans, her favorite socks with spades on them and black boots with a few buckles on each.

As she exited the house five minutes later with the bag draped over her shoulders and down her back, Lee nodded to her. He turned and headed toward the fountain with Mallory at his heels. Queen Evana sat upon the fountain in the beautiful rays of the sun waiting for them. The day was warm and a small southern breeze was a perfect accessory to such a beautiful day.

Upon approaching the queen Lee bowed his head as was tradition for all elven men and women to do. Mallory did likewise, showing respect for the woman who not only gave her a place to sleep the previous night but also the woman who would explain to her the only way for her to return to Earth – her Earth. Everything was still such a mystery to her. She was in a foreign land that would only become ever stranger the more she ventured into it. She had no idea that what she had seen so far was mild compared to the complex ideologies and exotic creatures she would come across on her travels. Her mouth opened and shut almost instantly.

"Hello Mallory, hello Lee," the elven queen stated kindly with a smile. Altruistic in nature, Queen Evana never failed to make her subjects smile and feel cared for. It helped that her skin was naturally smooth and wrinkle-free allowing for a strange feeling of security to envelop anyone around her – except for maybe her enemies.

"Good morning, my queen," Lee said dropping to one knee before rising. Mallory followed suit.

"Good morning, your majesty." This was the first time in her life that Mallory had ever been in the presence of true royalty. It was a form of government she was not used to, but had the common courtesy and natural decency to pick up on rather quickly.

"You must be full of questions, Mallory. I will answer as many as I possibly can, but there may be some I don't have an answer too. I want you to understand this possibility before you begin asking. There are many things I know, but there are still many things I do not." Evana's gaze never left Mallory's. Her very stare seemed to suck the soul out of you. Its grip was powerful.

"Yes, your majesty. I understand and will take whatever information and answers you can give to me. I'm very grateful for the help." She turned and stared at Lee who looked down at her and nodded his head showing approval for the questions he knew she was about to ask. She turned back towards the queen and continued: "All I wish is to get back to my father, hopefully with the purist water to help cure the fatal disease that eats away at his very existence." Her fists clenched at the thought but she relaxed them again. "Lee has told me where we must travel to find this water. But how will I bring it back with me?"

"The water may be held inside this capsule." Evana stood and lifted a vial with a silver chain attached to it from her lap. "Once in possession, keep the Water of Tears around your neck and close to your heart."

"Water of Tears?" Mallory asked.

"Yes, that is the true name of the purist water," Evana recounted and wrapped the vial necklace around Mallory's neck tying it in the back. Mallory wrapped her hand around the vial and then tucked it inside her shirt between her breasts.

"How do I return to Earth from this land?"

"In the center of this world lies a kingdom called 'Caidel', where there are creatures called the Humanus and they are Everworld's version of the human race. Their likeness to that of Earth's humans is almost eerie. The only difference lies in distinct visual characteristics such as eye and hair color. Their hair color is never that of straw nor their eyes that of the sky."

"So, there are no blonde or blue-eyed Humanus in Caidel?" Mallory checked the facts.

"That is correct," Evana agreed. "They have in their possession the only other portal from this world to Earth. Guarded in their castle lies the copy of the same book you used to travel into our world. Their copy also has the same pendant that you now carry in your pocket." Her eyes never left Mallory's.

"How did you know…" Mallory began but was cut off.

"There are many things I know, and still many I don't," Evana calmly reminded Mallory and smiled.

Mallory thought for a second before asking her next question. She wanted to figure out how she could find out everything that Evana didn't know and what she'd have to find out on her own without guessing. The perfect question came to her mind and she opened her mouth to speak: "What do you not know, and what can you not tell me?"

Queen Evana stared into Mallory's eyes and searched as if trying to solve a puzzle. She never expected such an astute question from such a young individual. Mallory was more sagacious than Queen Evana anticipated, but this helped to ease her worry a little. Maybe, just maybe this shrewd teenaged girl could do a great deal more than Evana hoped.

Evana responded: "Along your journey you will face many challenges. I cannot tell you what they may be for I cannot see the future, and because of this I cannot tell you how to defeat or solve the problems that might arise. I cannot tell you that everything will work out in your favor as much as I desire it to. I do not know if this water will fix your father's ailment for it is not of his world."

"So, this may be all for nothing?" Mallory's voice was soft and she wrapped her hand back around the vial thinking of the unfortunate possibilities.

"It's possible," the queen agreed. "But you never know if you never try." Her hands wrapped around Mallory's left hand.

"I know we've been given canteens for water," Mallory stated, "but what will we do for food."

"Food will be collected on your travels. There is much safe wild vegetation in Everworld along with other consumables. There are wild creatures such as deer. Your father had very similar questions regarding food which is why I have these answers for you. We do not have deer exactly but the creatures are similar in structure regarding nutrients such as protein. Wild grains also grow sporadically in Everworld. Food will be available most everywhere you go. Lee can help you determine what is safe to eat and what is not."

"Thank you, so much," Mallory repeated. "I believe you have answered everything I can think of at the moment. If other questions arise I will consult Lee… Oh!" Mallory exclaimed. "I forgot to ask. How will we travel? Will it all be by foot or are there modes of transportation here?"

"In our village there is none, other than cloppers."

"Cloppers?" Mallory looked confusingly at Evana.

"Your father compared them to what he called horses, I believe it was," Evana responded.

"I probably wouldn't be able to ride them then," Mallory decided. "So, on foot it is. Thank goodness for these boots I'm wearing." She looked down at the black leather covering her feet and then back up at the queen. "I'm ready to go." She turned to Lee. Lee looked at her and let out a small smile. He was rough around the edges but underneath the tough exterior Mallory could tell Lee was a gentle elf.

"Good luck, my thoughts will be with you on your travels. Remember, not all of Everworld is safe, so please, travel with caution," Evana warned.

"I promise my queen," Lee said and crossed his right arm over his chest. This was their version of a salute Mallory figured.

"Goodbye, fair queen."

"Follow the path behind you until you come to a fork in the road," Evana began. "From there the decisions will be yours. That is all the directional advice I can give."

"The decision will be yours, Mallory, unless I believe you are taking us way off course," Lee said. Mallory nodded. Both Mallory and Lee filled their canteens with water from the fountain they stood by and turned to walk away. Lee's strides were a bit longer than Mallory's so keeping up would be a bit harder for her. They walked away, with their backs to the queen and the city of Algernon with their beautiful hand-carved homes and caring queen.

On my mark, get set, go, Mallory thought as they took off.

After about ten minutes of walking out of the lovely little town the pair came to their first decision. A fork in the path split the road in two very different directions. A sign sat stuck in the ground in the middle of the fork with arrows pointing two ways and writing on each arrow.

One read: Northwest – The Black Forrest Hills

The other read: Northeast – The Valley of Shadows

Lee spoke for the first time since their departure. "The Black Forrest Hills is the easier way to the Silver Lake. There is more danger but the danger is less severe. The Valley of Shadow provides less danger, but the danger has the potential to be more severe. The choice is yours. I will protect you the best I can if any bad situation arises, as promised."

Mallory thought for a second. Her eyes twitched as if searching her brain for what the best decision would be. She thought about her father, how bad she wanted to save him. How she would do anything for him. What she believed he would do. She thought about how nothing in her life had been easy this far, and how she'd never taken the easy way out of anything, so why start now? The toughness she faced along the path she chose would only make her stronger, if she survived at all.

Back at home on Earth Michael was staring into the pages of the book as words magically appeared as Mallory and Lee's story unfolded physically in the clear air and beautiful sunshine of Everworld.

"Mallory," Michael said, "please, choose the Valley of Shadows." He gripped the book tighter in his grasp. "No matter which path you take I'll be here with you every step of the way. I know you don't know, but I do. I'm very proud of you and proud to be your father." Tears formed in his eyes.

"The Valley of Shadows," Mallory said and turned and stared up into Lee's eyes. "I want to go northeast." Her voice was firm and unwavering. Lee nodded down to her and they both turned right and headed to the Valley of Shadows.

Michael, still reading along, smiled down at the book and said, "That's my girl."

Clouds began to form far off in the distance. It would be another multitude of hours before they arrived at the plains, and Mallory would force Lee into conversation, something he was so very unused to.

Chapter 8

DARK WATER, DARK WEST

A crow cries out at the crack of night's noon.
Watch for the raven, he's coming soon.
Dark water falls at trust's lagoon.

Lullabies can bless or curse the entire dreamscape of a child. A good dream – sometimes called a fantasy – leaves one usually feeling safe, happy and secure. Problems can be solved and personal struggles either fade away or genuinely don't exist. Unfortunately, and realistically, not every dream can be a good one. Not every fisherman can catch the legend. Sometimes, the fisherman is the bait. Sometimes, the legend catches him. So, yes, sometimes the monsters are real, very, very real. It's when a nightmare becomes reality that the true problems arise. The real gets pushed aside and the all-too-real begins.

A half-moon dimly lit a landscape coated in a thin layer of chocolate-brown mud and small patches of green sprouted from the watered-down dirt in little patches polka-dotting the area. Footprints in a variety of sizes turned the surface into a giant jigsaw puzzle while up above crystal stars shimmered brightly in a satin-black sky.

This Muddy Hills region is the home of the Centrions. They stayed as far away from the other species of Everworld as possible and trusted none except their own. The Dark Queen was an exception due to her dominant attitude and selfish desires that resonated with the Centrions. Not all Centrions trusted or even liked the queen, but their warlord leader and head honcho, Krum, did. Krum believed that, with the Dark Queen at their side and their military might, nothing could stop them from taking over the entire realm of Everworld. As a war-mongering species they believed that survival was based on power and dominance rather than peace. In fact, the Centrions don't believe in personal relationships or love. They only procreate as a species as a survival tactic. So far it had worked for them and worked well.

A crow drifted down from the darkness that shrouded the landscape and landed softly upon the top point of a boulder with moss growing on its visible underside. The crow let out a squawk as it cried into the night spreading it wings and twitching its head left and right. It sat there and watched the two approaching Centrions as they made their way past the boulder with the big, black bird perched on top.

"Drayt, if what you're saying is true we haven't much time," the bigger of the two Centrions said. He held a spear in one hand and sunk the bottom of the shaft into the thick mud underneath.

"True it is. Krum told me that Queen Anna's orb was clouded in a dark smoke that wouldn't let her see," Drayt said. A large metal shield with round bosses formed in a circle on the inside perimeter hung by his side, his right arm tucked inside one of the enarmes of the shield while his right fist closed around the other.

"Why would the orb disobey the queen? What is so secretive about this new stranger to our land that even one of the most powerful sorceresses can't see who it is?"

"That's what intrigues Krum. It intrigues us all, Gilf," Drayt responded as the crow atop the boulder let out another squawk. Both Centrions ignored the warning.

Gilf's eyes dropped to the ground as he thought. "So, what do we do? Do we continue to play along until we know who this new threat is and then take action depending?" Gilf rubbed the back of his neck with his giant hand that was covered in a thick layer of boar hair. His eyes returned to Drayt's.

"The rest of our men have no idea and they won't until the time is right, correct?" Drayt's eyes intensified making sure that this valuable information stayed locked up within the lips and mind of Gilf.

"Yes," came Gilf's response and he proceeded to stand at attention as if giving a salute causing the staff of his spear to become unstuck from the mud.

Off in the distance the small roaring of a waterfall added an atmospheric rumble to the already turbulent situation that brought the two Centrions to the Dark Falls in the first place. Plans for a Centrion domination of Everworld were clearly in the works and these two generals of Krum's army were the leaders behind the main man himself. His most trusted allies, Drayt and Gilf, had been with him through many battles and even fought beside him in the last war. They saw a great potential within the Centrion troops. This was the greatest military that Everworld had ever seen. If it wasn't for the sheer numbers of their enemies and the bravery of Michael Bones it's undoubted that the previous war would have ended with a much different outcome. The Centrions numbers had grown exponentially since then. They also had younger and stronger warriors to work with. Something about the time just seemed right.

The two generals made their way to the rushing water that cascaded out of one of the caves dug naturally into the mountain from springs from long ago. As they listened to the water that flooded out of the mountain's core they looked to the sky at the brightness of the moon. Wolves, a rare creature in Everworld, howled in the distance. The Dark Falls served as the nucleus to the dark west – a nickname for the westernmost part of Everworld that was always covered in trees and saw very little sunlight. Scads of mountains created a plethora of shadows within the few valleys that inhabited the region. Even the ocean that lay nestled at the bottom of the western cliff's edges was a darker blue than that of the east. It was like night and day. The purple and indigo waters of the west held their own secrets and were home to many creatures that only the most adventurous of individuals came across. These were the kind of waters where myths were born. Tales of giant beasts that rose from the sea and mangled your vessel were among the most common of these rare tales, but none could forget the tale of old Captain Shax who went to his grave with his one wooden leg and swore on the vision of his standalone eye about the day he saw the beauty of the sea. Not only did the mermaid save him from drowning the day his boat was destroyed but also swam him back to shore after he passed out. That storm was a doozy, and some say so are his tales.

"What do you think is out there?" Gilf stated as his beady eyes peered into the sea of stars hovering above them.

"What do you mean?" Drayt snorted as he looked questioningly at the face of Gilf that was still locked onto the sky.

"Those bright things in the sky that we call stars," Gilf started, his snout erect to the vast blackness above. "Where do they come from? They just appear at night. We know very little but from what the Humanus have discovered – as absurd and tastelessly incredible as they are – their telescope technology allows them to see into the skies and have been able to positively dictate and confirm that the stars are other worlds. I wonder what else is out there sometimes." Gilf lowered his eyes to meet Drayt's who furred his brow in disbelief.

"We're on the brink of creating war and taking over an entire world and your thoughts are about what other worlds might be like? I would smack you if you weren't so hilarious." Drayt's voice, which held an accent close to that of Earth's Australian, was deep and heavy. His fist jutted out at a slow speed and playfully collided with the broad mass that was Gilf's shoulder. Gilf laughed along with Drayt.

The big, black crow that was perched atop the boulder a ways back came fluttering down out of the sky again and let out another one if it's ear-curling songs. It landed near the feet of the generals and squawked again.

"I'm getting real tired of you," Gilf said before shifting his spear around in his hand and poked it fiercely at the crow. The crow suddenly jumped up toward his face and with its hooked feet and sharp nails began scratching at Gilf's eyes. Gilf cried out: "Damn bird! You little bastard!" and waved his arms in front of his face to shoo the bird off. "What the hell was that?"

"I'm not sure. Something obviously pissed in its crumb cake though," Drayt added with a small, hoarse laugh.

"It's not funny," Gilf scolded.

Water continued to rush out of the mountain cove behind the two Centrions as they sat in silence. Drayt plunged his thick, hairy fingers into the plunge pool that lay at the bottom of the waterfall. Ripples bounced out from around their edges in little rings that gradually became larger. A cremmol's cry came from deep within the woods that lay not even fifty yards beyond the waterfall and its bottom basin. Cremmol's were small enough but they were mean creatures. They had the size of a badger but the tenacity of a raccoon. Drayt and Gilf turned their attention towards the dark woods that, at night, seemed somehow even darker than normal.

"You know," Drayt began, "sometimes I can't tell what's more terrifying."

"Between what?" Gilf asked.

"The cremmol's death cry or your face in the morning." Both began laughing before they agreed to go back to their village and call it a night. They followed their large footprints back in the light of the moon as the stars danced and sparkled overhead.

Trust in their leader was all they had to go on, but trust is a brittle substance. The smallest crack can turn into a cavern over a period of time or even at a moment's notice. It all depends on the severity of the something that caused the crack in the first place. On both of their minds was the recent conversation and what may lie ahead within the next few days. One advantage they had was already knowing something wasn't right – that was far more information than Mallory, Lee, or even Queen Evana had. They walked in silence and let the calm breeze that rustled the leaves of the dark forest do all the talking. At least heading back to the village was heading away from the dark woods and from whatever had killed the cremmol.

Chapter 9

ALL THE QUEEN'S ARMY AND ALL THE QUEEN'S MEN

Love conquers all, even that of gory war;
Soft, shifting in the heart
Brings out glory worth fighting for
Not a budge, dark heart
Amass, legions score;
Unafraid of death's cold grip
Leads an army door to door

Darkness swallowed the outside and inside of Westershire Castle. Only candles dimly lit the large rooms that were now covered by thick, black drapes. More often than not a large amount and assortment of candles would be lit to help the queen see more clearly. Her eyesight was fine, but it was nowhere near comparable to that of the Centrions with their ability to see in the dark.

"Krum," she stood from her throne and walked over to one of the windows carved into the turret and slid back the heavy drape uncovering a nightscape she had come to hold dear to her heart. Krum dropped to a knee and crossed his right arm over his chest.

"Yes my queen?"

"A feeling has been growing inside me that I can no longer ignore. There is something wrong," she paused before facing her body back to the room. Krum stood up and looked directly into her eyes while the moon cast a glint of light off her dark hair.

"What do you fear is the problem?" Like a good commander he never took his eyes off hers without her permission.

"It doesn't make any sense, but I don't know how else to describe it." She closed her hand around the "M" necklace that gripped her neck. "When I first felt something was wrong I looked into the glass to find nothing more than a foggy picture, however, in my heart I felt a stir. Something became unsettled." She closed her eyes and let her hand drop back to her sides

"What do you believe this entails, your majesty?" Krum narrowed his eyes in concentration.

"It feels like a piece of me is out there in Everworld, but that's impossible. I want someone to look into this." She opened her eyes that pierced the air like a dart in Krum's direction. "This calls for rather drastic measures. I'm sure of it."

"My queen," Krum responded without the slightest quiver.

"Bring me the Magician," Evelyn commanded.

Krum descended the old, stone staircase that spiraled down into the dungeons of Westershire. Only the worst of criminals or those who posed the greatest threat to royalty were interred down here. These old cell walls only held one inhabitant these days: the

Magician. The Magician used to be Evelyn's jester and before that he spent his days honing his craft and magic powers under the watchful eyes of King Destin and Queen Lizabeth. When Azaroth attempted to take over Westershire, he recruited the Magician to help him, but eventually the Magician was captured with the help of Azarim and Michael Bones right after Azaroth's disappearance. The Magician's black heart became even darker when his supposed ally left him to the devices of Azarim and Michael. His last thirty years in captivity have only hardened the evil inside his heart and infused the grim into his bones. For some reason Queen Anna's powers were being blocked, but just maybe the Magician's powers could clear the image inside the crystal ball and bring forth the identity of the mysterious traveler.

Up until this point the Magician was kept in a weak state or else he'd easily have overpowered the Centrions that kept watch over him. Luckily, over the years his powers had weakened from his forced abstention of the use of magic to a state that was much weaker than the queen's. She could control him with ease though his intelligence never dwindled. He was still as cunning as ever. His midnight hair had also grown very long as it had not been cut the entirety of his captivity. A long, black beard had also formed along his strong jaw-line. Boney fingers linked together as he lay quietly in his cell bed. A rattling of keys disturbed the quiet still of the chamber as a metal key slid into an old lock.

"Old man," Krum's voice was rough. "Queen Anna has requested an audience with you." Humming from inside the cell came to a halt.

A voice that hadn't been heard in over two decades echoed off the cold, stone walls, "Oh? After twenty-eight years why does she want to see me?" He coughed as he hadn't spoken in quite some time. It was odd hearing his own voice out loud instead of just inside his head.

"That is her business to tell. Come!" Krum demanded and without a moment's hesitation the Magician came. Krum shackled together his hands and feet and lead him up the dark, twisting staircase to a dimly lit room which held the throne and the presence of the queen herself.

The Magician's old eyes hurt from even the faint light of the fires that bathed the room in a soft glow but he battled through the dull pain to look into the eyes of the woman who had been his jailer for what seemed like an eternity.

"Magician," the Dark Queen began as Krum swept his feet out from under him and pushed him to his knees. "Krum, allow him to stand," she stated as Krum brought him back to his feet. "Magician," she began again, "what is your true name?"

The Magician let out a small laugh and answered, "After twenty-eight years you request an audience with me to ask my name?"

Krum swung his arm back to strike the Magician but the Dark Queen raised hers to motion Krum to pause and spoke. "Recent happenings have occurred where I may be in need of your services, and I can make it worth your while. Depending on how well you serve these needs rewards can range all the way up to that of freedom." A glint lit quickly in the eyes of the Magician. "So, I ask only once more: What is your name?"

"I have no name, at least none I can remember. I am known only as the Magician. I tell you this with all the truth in my heart." His eyes never left hers as a sign of honesty. She could sense this was so.

"Then I shall call you Magician for now. Come up with a name for yourself and I will call you that when the time becomes appropriate. Take it as an offering for your assistance and future help and more freedoms and payments will come your way." The Magician nodded in agreement.

"What does your majesty request of me?" The Magician's old eyes continued to stare directly into the cold stare of the Dark Queen's.

"Someone has come to this world – a traveler. My crystal ball is only showing me blurry images and shadows. No matter what I do I can't get it to give me a clear picture of who this traveler is. Not only that, I feel something is wrong. It's like a stir in my heart. I want you to make these pictures clear."

"That can be done," the Magician promised, "but not in my current state, for I haven't performed magic in years. The state my body and mind are currently in is terrible and weak. I ask for just a week of nutrition and restful sleep. Please allow me to obtain a little of my power back and this task you ask of me will be done without any problems or limitations. You and I both know that only a couple days of rest and nutrition are not enough to allow me to surpass you in power. For I cannot surpass your power even with months or years of training," he bowed his head. "Therefore, I shall pose no threat – not that I could, either way, my queen – as I gather enough strength to perform this task you desire of me. Please," he added at the end with his head still bowed.

After a moment of inner thought and deliberation the queen answered: "It shall be so. Krum, please escort the Magician to his new quarters and station two guards on the door." She turned back to the Magician. "I trust you realize that any attempt to disobey or fight against my wishes will result in your automatic execution?"

"Understood, my Queen," the Magician calmly stated and bowed again before being shoved through the doors by Krum.

"Drayt? Gilf?" The Dark Queen turned to face the two generals. "Krum tells me that the Centrion Army has grown two-fold over the course of the last five years."

"Yes, my queen." Both generals answered in unison and stood at attention at the sound of their queen's voice.

"Good. At the end of this current cycle I expect everything to be ready and the first phase of our attacks to begin." She paused and turned back toward the open window and stared out into the cool night. "I've waited a long time for this." A fire spark lit within her eyes and it was by far the brightest light inside the darkness of the night.

Chapter 10

WARRIORS OF PRIDE

*Warriors of Pride
In the Valley of the Sun
Shadows tell a tale*

"What do you think?" Mallory turned to Lee and looked up into his eyes smiling. She was becoming more comfortable around him as they worked their way northeast on the grounds of Everworld.

"I think you like to talk and you ask many questions," Lee responded as he looked down into the eyes of the smiling youth. "However," he continued, "I also believe that you look for answers in attempts to gain intelligence and I find that to be very wise, especially considering the circumstances surrounding your current predicaments," he finished as they came over a ridge and looked out onto a large savannah. This stretch of grassland seemed to flow on for miles before giving birth to a wall of mountains that encircled it.

Down in the large grasslands quite some distance away some buildings could be seen along with a few animals. These buildings seemed to resemble that of the Native American style she saw in her history classes and read about in some books back on Earth. Some of the animals she could make out from the distance seemed awfully familiar. Some appeared to look nearly identical to that of Earth's horses. Every part of their body seemed to be the same except for the head which seemed to resemble that of a steer. "These must be the cloppers that Queen Evana mentioned back in Algernon," she told herself. Mallory looked to her left and saw some animals that resembled bison. "What are those over there, Lee? They looked like an animal called bison on Earth."

"Those are called sahk-kahs," Lee answered honestly. "They were first discovered by the people of these plains, so out of respect, we call them the name the native warriors of these grasslands gave them," he added.

A large bird flew overhead and let out a mighty shriek. It looked like a mix between an eagle and a falcon. Mallory was in awe at its majesty as it glided gracefully in the air for what seemed like a mile or two.

"That thing was huge!" Mallory exclaimed.

"That," Lee countered, "was a faracaw. They are a mighty species of bird that are the only match for the griffins that reside in the mountainous regions of Everworld."

"Could this be the land that mythical bird comes from?" Mallory asked herself. "Are griffins…" she paused and thought for the right word before finishing, "… dangerous?"

"They are the most likely to attack, other than the broadwings." Lee took his bow off his back but kept the arrows aside and placed the faracaw in his crosshairs as a hunter would practice for a shot.

"Broadwings?" Mallory looked puzzled.

"They are scavengers. Naked-headed creatures with ruffles around their neck."

"They sound like vultures," Mallory explained.

"Vultures?" The word left Lee's mouth with a weird taste. "You Earthlings have the funniest names for your animals," Lee stated.

"We do," she thought sarcastically to herself. "How about 'cloppers' or 'faracaws'?" She huffed to herself.

Lee replaced his weapon and turned to Mallory. "These lands are known as the Pride Lands throughout all of Everworld. These Pride Lands have another name, 'The Valley of Shadows'. It receives that name because of all the shadows that get cast within these grasslands. There are no trees or rocks, except for near the bottom of the mountains, as you can see, to block the sun giving everything a shadow that enters it. The Valley of Shadows is home to the ruthless and strong Natarian warrior race. They are a very observant people and don't take kindly to strangers invading their lands. They must always be aware, especially with living in such open land, but they're strong enough to handle themselves. They are a smart people that understand how to live off the land and they travel and hunt in numbers."

Mallory nodded in understanding and noticed a small grove of trees near what appeared to be a small lake and figured that must be where they sourced their wood to make their homes and other shelters. They also sourced their stones there too. She figured water must fall from the mountains and keep the lake from drying up.

Back on Earth Michael read along as Mallory continued her quest to the Silver Lake. He knew he wouldn't be able to follow every single step of her journey but figured he'd get in what he could. If something was happening to his daughter he wanted to know – after all, he was her father. He couldn't believe that his daughter was experiencing

Everworld in the first place. He thought he had rid himself of that place and never suspected his daughter would come stumbling across it. But, he figured it made him stronger as a human being and that his daughter would come out for the better too after her journey had completed. He just hoped Lee could truly keep her safe.

As Michael read along with Mallory looking down on the Valley of Shadows, it sparked memories within his head and heart. His first encounter with the Natarians wasn't the most pleasant but after the unpleasantries had passed he was glad to have met the tribesmen and women who made his experience in Everworld that much better. He would go on to fight alongside these brave men and women warriors during the war and unfortunately lose a lot of friends he had made along the way. The majority of the elder folk had either perished during the war or passed from old age by this point. He figured the eldest member couldn't be more than sixty.

"Lee, wherever this trip takes you two, please keep my daughter safe," Michael said aloud as he read along with Mallory's actions and experiences.

"Mallory Bones," Lee said as he turned Mallory firmly by the shoulders to stare down into her eyes. "We must pass through the Valley of Shadows to continue our journey to the Silver Lake. Our only other option is to turn around and head back toward the Black Forrest Hills. If you decide to continue forward into the Valley of Shadows be forewarned, the Natarians don't take kindly to strangers as I mentioned before. If you even try to talk out of turn I cannot tell you what consequences may occur. So, for your safety, do as I say and keep quiet until I talk first, no matter what they say or do. This is very crucial. Do you understand?" Lee's words were spoken calmly but firmly.

Mallory looked intently into Lee's eyes that showed no signs of false truths. "I promise." Lee nodded and the pair then set off down the decline into the grasslands and towards the surprise that awaited them.

Four figures riding on cloppers approached the two stragglers as they passed the three-quarter mark between the decline they started from and the first structures built by the Natarians. Mallory and Lee were still about a mile from reaching the nearest structures but that didn't stop the four figures from approaching them this far out with great caution.

As the four riders came closer Mallory could make out that there were two men and two women. All were very muscular and had similar physical features. Thick, heavy, dark red hair flowed from their heads and traced the broad shoulders and curved muscular bodies that were wrapped in tight, tan skin. They all appeared tall. Even though they sat atop the cloppers their height was unmistakable. They had to be at least six feet in height Mallory guessed.

The riders circled them; one of the females approached a step closer aboard her steed and spoke: "En ning-gah." Mallory looked to Lee who stood silently. "Who are you?" She spoke again, this time in English, or at least what sounded like English to Mallory. Lee stood firm and quiet as he stared up at the riders then toward Mallory whose mouth opened but quickly shut upon her remembrance of what she promised Lee. "Speak now or you will be detained as our prisoner for trespassing on our lands." Still Lee stood silent as Mallory, confused, kept her mouth shut tight.

The two male riders proceeded to unmount and grab Lee by the arms. They stripped him of his bow, quiver, and arrows along with his canteen. The other female rider unmounted her clopper and did the same to Mallory who made no effort to fight back as Lee had not.

"By order of our law you are being detained. You have until the time of the high sun tomorrow to speak. If you refuse, you will be considered spies or scouts from another race and executed."

Mallory's eyes grew wide with terror as Lee turned to her and blinked as if to communicate. He uttered only one sentence, "I shall not speak to you, only to your high chief."

"The high chief will be at the execution, as he attends all executions. You have no right to see him before then. If that's not good enough then your death will be your choice as we gave you a chance before." She shot a look at Mallory, who wanted badly to speak, but trusted Lee and kept silent. It's all she had. She remembered what he said about unknown consequences and realized her only chance for survival was to follow his instructions. Lee and Mallory were placed atop the cloppers with their respective gendered detainer. The four riders, Lee and Mallory made their way towards the village.

As they arrived at the village Lee and Mallory were brought directly to a solid building surrounded by a group of large male and female Natarian warriors. They passed by many smaller dwellings that Mallory made out to be houses. Lee kept his gaze straight ahead and focused on personal thoughts. Many Natarian wore intrigued looks upon their faces as Mallory and Lee were led past. A small child with bright blue eyes stared at Mallory as she passed while hiding halfway behind someone. Mallory couldn't help but notice his stare as they rounded a corner in the path that led to their captive quarters.

Mallory and Lee dismounted the cloppers when instructed and were forced into what would be their prison for the night. The same warrior who spoke to them upon their arrival spoke to them now. "Tonight you will stay here until your execution tomorrow. You will have one more chance then to speak. If you choose to ignore these warnings, we will have no choice but to consider you spies or scouts for another army. You come to our land and speak nothing to us in any language. Suspicions are roused and will stay high." She gave them one more strong look before heading out of the building and rejoining the riders she was with prior to Mallory and Lee's capture.

The two adventurers settled into their makeshift prison as dusk settled outside. The sun had gone down behind the horizon creating a blanket of soft shade over the land. No clouds could be seen but that would surely change by morning. The temperature cooled down out here in the grasslands Mallory soon came to figure out. The cooler weather was a nice change from the brutal sun that left a small sunburn on the back of her neck. Mallory would spend the rest of the night thinking of her sick father and how worried he must be because of her disappearance. She wouldn't sleep at all that night. The same held true for Lee who was up all night thinking of the best way out of this situation. He almost couldn't bear to look at Mallory out of shame. He promised to keep her safe and he felt like he was failing. He knew a predicament like this called for drastic measures. He looked around his holdings and realized trying to escape was pointless as guards continued to hang around the prison quarters, so he walked over to Mallory who had a stream of tears flowing from her eyes and whispered something into her ear. The tears slowed to a halt and she nodded to him.

Back at home Michael tried to stay awake as he battled exhaustion, but he was even more terrified of falling asleep and missing the most crucial point of his daughter's adventure to date. He knew how the Natarians could be, and every minute that passed brought Mallory closer to possible death which worried him all the more. All he could do was what Mallory could do and place his trust in Lee. He spent the rest of his evening sitting in his favorite reading chair in the living room and looking at old photos of her growing up throughout the years while waiting for time to pass.

The quiet and thought-filled hours of night passed and daylight was beginning to pour over the Valley of Shadows. The sun remained hidden behind a wall of clouds and the first few drops of rain began to fall. The sprinkle grew into a steady shower eventually turning to rain as the Valley of Shadows became a valley of mud and water. Mallory and Lee were greeted by the same female warrior who first approached and spoke to them before they were restrained and brought out to a small structure in the middle of the village. It was tall and created by pillars and spikes of wood tethered together by vine and rope. Mallory and Lee's hands were tied separately to the structure as the rain continued to pour over them. A small group of six warriors formed a line in front of them each holding a bow with arrows. They kept dry, standing under another structure made of dense wood and leaves. The whole village seemed gathered to watch the impending execution. After Mallory and Lee were tied down the high chief of the village appeared before their eyes and sat upon a large throne to watch the execution of these two suspicious and quiet beings.

Back on Earth Michael fought against the exhaustion that plagued his body. He cared about no one more than his daughter and did what he had to do to see his daughter get through this safely – or so he hoped with all his heart. He took a deep breath and read on as the time of the execution narrowed down to the final few seconds before the arrows would fly, skewering Mallory and Lee and leaving nothing behind but memories and broken dreams.

Chapter 11

THE CHILD WITH THE SAPPHIRE EYES

Piercing like an arrow, sapphire blue
Locking on, never fleeting
Holding firm, warmly greeting
Always learning new, intellectual they grow

A crowd gathered around as a restrained Mallory and Lee stared into the muddy ground beneath their feet. Their arms were spread and their legs tied together and their heads hung low. Rain fell slowly as drops dripped from their soaked cheeks and chins.

"Do you have any final words?" The lady warrior who first spoke to them spoke once again before uttering what she believed would be the final words they would ever hear. Lee took in one last breath. He stared directly into the eyes of the high chief before his eyes hit the ground for a final time. Mallory's soft cries could be heard. She trusted Lee and now he was going to let her die. She couldn't let this happen so she opened her mouth to speak but no words came.

The high chief gripped the edge of the arm rests of his throne with his hands as he waited these final moments out. He noticed Mallory's mouth open out of the corner of his eye and his head twitched in her direction.

"They seem to abjure," the female warrior said again. She turned toward the firing squad. "Raise your arrows. Ninka." She turned to face another female who scratched a torch to light. "Set them ablaze." Ninka did as instructed and lit all six arrows. Three aimed toward Mallory and three aimed toward Lee. Only a small cry escaped from Mallory's tight throat. "Take aim." The female warrior raised her arm, but the minute her arm reached its pinnacle is when Lee spoke for the first time since their capture.

"Ym eman…" Lee's voice was deep but held no quiver. Rain drops dripped off the tip of his nose and ears as he slowly lifted his head. He had a stone cold gaze as he stared right into the eyes of the high chief. He spoke again, "Ym eman, Lee." Mallory, even more speechless than before, if that was possible, stared at Lee who seemed to be speaking a different language if a language at all. After a few moments she noticed her mouth hung rudely open so she proceeded to close it.

The high chief sat straight up in his chair at the sound of Lee's words. He turned to the female warrior and spoke, "Ahawi, Dun-tah-nu-wah!" He swung his hand slowly downward. Ahawi turned toward the firing squad.

"Lower your weapons," she spoke to them with firm authority.

Back on Earth Michael let out a deep breath he had been holding in, his face turning red with anger, sadness and a whole bucket of emotions that all spilled out at once. He closed his eyes and lay back, resting the book on his chest, pages facing down. He watched his little girl grow up at the speed of light within his mind and now he would be able to continue to watch her grow, at least until the cancer took him first. "Thank you, Lee," he said in a whispered tone before he took one more deep breath then opened his eyes and flipped the book back right-side up.

In Everworld, the high chief spoke: "These two shall not be harmed. I must speak to them. He speaks in the tongue of old. There is little to no chance he is an enemy." The high chief turned toward Lee. "Do you speak the universal tongue as well?"

"Yes, high chief," came Lee's response.

"Lee," At the mention of Lee's name Mallory's eyes widened. "Where do you hail from and who is the young woman who accompanies you?"

"I promise that all will be answered if you release us. We are no threat." Their locked eyes never diverted from each other's stare.

The high chief sat for a moment before nodding and turned toward Ahawi. He motioned for her to release them and she did as he commanded. Upon release Mallory and Lee rubbed their wrists and moved very carefully so as to not give reason for false alarm. He waved them over and they proceeded toward him slowly, keeping their hands visible at all times. When they reached the foot of his thrown Lee bowed and fell to one knee and pulled Mallory with him.

"High chief," Lee began as he knelt before the leader of the Natarians, "My full name is Lee Odion, my companion's name is Mallory Bones…"

"Bones?" the high chief interrupted and Mallory nodded her head.

"Yes, sir," she responded.

"Are you kin of the one named Michael Bones," he asked.

"Yes," Mallory answered. "He is my father."

At the sound of this answer he raised both her and Lee to their feet and bowed to Mallory who stood silently in shock. "Mallory Bones, I knew your father very well. My name is Annikan Tawah; I am the high chief of these valleys and the Natarian people of Everworld. I'm sorry for the way you were treated but we are very protective of our lands. Ever since the last Great War we have done what is necessary to protect them from being invaded and taken over. Ahawi is our head warrior and she serves us well. She only follows the laws of our land."

"We Elves of Algernon have similar laws in regards to random travelers coming through our lands. We are sorry for passing through your valley without permission, high chief, but we are on an important mission to the Silver Lake up in the northern territories. We must gather a small portion of the Water of Tears. Michael Bones is back on Earth dying from the Final Death. Mallory looks to gather just enough to cure him. She chose to come this way rather than travel through the Black Forrest Hills. I am her guard along this journey." He then turned toward Mallory and bent to one knee. "I am so sorry, Mallory Bones. I had no choice but to wait until the final moment to speak in front of the high chief. I spoke a language only a very few know. It's an old language that almost died along with all the elders during the war thirty years ago. I knew that if I spoke this language he would consider us no threat. Very few speak this language anymore. The language the Natarians speak now is newly developed." He turned back towards Chief Annikan.

"Mallory Bones, please accept my apology." Annikan bowed his head.

"It's okay. I'm a stranger to not only these lands but also to your world. It's only normal that you would be wary of my intentions," Mallory replied.

"What is your age?" Annikan asked.

"I'm sixteen," Mallory responded realizing that this was the first time she had been asked this question.

"Does your father know you are here?" Annikan asked. "In Everworld," he added.

"No," Mallory lost focus again. "I was transported into this world through accident. I was in a bookstore back on Earth when I found this old book and took it home. I noticed the symbol on the cover could be detached so I took it off and when I reopened the book while holding onto the detached symbol, I was transported to a temple in a forest near Algernon. That's when Lee found me." She turned toward Lee who looked at her and smiled. She regained focus. "I'm just trying to get home with the cure for my father."

"I understand," Chief Annikan said with his hands together over his chest. "The road to the Silver Lake can be dangerous. I know not of Lee's abilities, and I mean no disrespect as the elven people are very tenacious and strong-willed, but would you like another warrior to assist you in your quest for protection? I can have one of my warriors come with you to help guide you on your quest."

Mallory turned toward Lee who simply nodded down to her with a smile and closed his eyes. "That is your choice, Mallory. My duty is simply to protect you and help you fulfill this mission. The elven people owe a great deal to Michael Bones for the services he provided during the war and for the peace he brought back to Everworld."

"As do the new generations of Natarians," Chief Annikan added. "Would you like another to join you? I promise that my warriors are strong and courageous. They will not fail you."

"Yes," Mallory answered and bowed. "I'm very grateful for such a generous offer."

"Would you like to hear more stories of how your father fought bravely alongside some of our greatest warriors?" Annikan asked as he motioned for Mallory and Lee to follow him to his home: a large wigwag-style structure.

"I'd love to!" Mallory responded and they spent the rest of the morning hearing more stories of the famous Michael Bones and cleaning up the execution site and the quarters where Mallory and Lee were held. On their way to Annikan Tawah's tent Mallory noticed a small child, the same child she had seen the day before that had hid behind its mother, run past them along the path and smile up at her before continuing on and disappearing behind a corner. She knew it was the same child. He had unmistakable eyes that reminded Mallory of sapphire blue.

Later that day Mallory and Lee were out enjoying the sunshine that appeared and dispersed the clouds. The Natarian's valleys were more than just grassland. They had statues dedicated to some of their warriors and heroes throughout their history. While taking a look at a statue dedicated to a warrior named Neeka Lo'Hota, Ahawi approached them and bowed before speaking: "Excuse me. I come to you to apologize and hope for forgiveness regarding the actions that have recently taken place."

Mallory took the initiative to respond to her almost cutting in immediately; "It's okay. You only followed orders and the laws of your people and that's very noble. It means a lot that you came to find us to apologize, though." She took Ahawi's hands in hers and smiled while staring into her eyes. She released Ahawi's hands and Ahawi smiled back.

"May I ask which warrior will be joining us?" Lee asked Ahawi.

"The second in command under me will be joining you. I must stay here and watch over the Valley of Shadows. His name is Koel Lo'Hota and yes, he is related to the warrior that statue is dedicated to right behind you. Koel is the grandson of Neeka." Just as Ahawi spoke the young child with the sapphire eyes came running up to her and hid halfway behind her but his gaze with his visible eye was locked onto Mallory.

"And who might you be?" Mallory said as she bent down to the child's height and looked into his eyes, her hands resting on her knees.

"This is Tokano, he is my son," Ahawi said, ruffling his dark hair with her hand. "Tokano come out and say hello." she ordered. Tokano came out slowly from behind her and walked up to Mallory, his little feet getting lost in the deep green grass that covered the Valley of Shadows.

"His eyes are so intense," Mallory admired and looked back towards Ahawi who was smiling.

"There are no other blue-eyed people in our lands. They are even bluer than yours, Mallory Bones."

"They are beautiful," Mallory said.

"To the Natarian people, your hair is even rarer. Nobody in the entirety of Everworld has the hair color of straw."

"Lee said the same thing to me," Mallory responded and Lee nodded in agreeance. "Thank you. My blonde hair comes from my mother. My father possesses light brown hair." Thoughts of her mother and father entered her head. She missed her mother and father dearly. Her heart sank at the thought of her mother and raced back up at the thought of her father. She closed her eyes and regained her focus. A light breeze lofted through the air and brushed her cheek. She swore she could hear her father's voice in the wind. A smirk crossed her face as she refocused on Ahawi.

"Chief Annikan has asked that you have dinner tonight with himself, Koel and me. Do you accept?" Ahawi looked at both Mallory and Lee. Lee looked toward Mallory who felt like the entire world was staring at her that instant.

"Graciously," Mallory responded. "Please send our thanks. What time shall we meet at the chief's home?"

"When the shadow of the large sundial in the center of our village points toward the statue of Neeka Lo'Hota the time for dinner will soon follow, so please head toward Annikan's home then. Until then, enjoy your stay in our village and please feel free to look around and take in the sights." Ahawi bowed one more time before turning and walking toward an undisclosed location. Tokano followed at her heels peering back over his shoulder before disappearing with Ahawi around a corner.

While the sun roasted high in the sky, tanning Mallory's skin and darkening Lee's even more, the pair decided to see what other history the village had to offer. Mallory and Lee walked by a few tents which seemed to be shopping tents. There were fresh foods which resembled fruits and Lee was able to explain what a few of them were to her. It was then that Mallory realized she didn't know what kind of currency Everworld had. Lee explained to her that there really wasn't a true form of currency and that mostly everyone just traded to get what they needed. Instead of traveling to a different world Mallory felt more like she had traveled back in time. As much fun as she was having in Everworld she wanted to get home that much faster because she knew time to save her father was running thin.

Chapter 12

A DIFFERENT SORT OF PLAN

Light and dark against themselves
A tale that time will tell,
The lowest at the top
Divide and unleash hell
Alliances once strong and true
Darken like the wood
Burn up into ashes, clashes bad and good.

Upon the highest hill that overlooked the rest of the Muddy Hills stood Drayt and Gilf, the two of the highest ranking generals of the Centrion Army. Beneath them, a sea of Centrions gathered in drones waiting to hear their superiors speak. The waves of lines went on for what seemed like hundreds of yards. These waves were split into rows and columns. In front of each platoon stood a captain and next to them stood a flag bearer. On each flag was a picture of a crest. Six platoons in all lined the fields. Each captain not only had their own distinct physical features but each was branded with the main symbol of their platoon's flag.

The captain's name of the platoon at the farthest left was Daragorn, followed by Gorga, Dragu, Stoval, Luga and Kaen stood on the far right. Daragorn was the tallest of the Centrion captains. Being the second longest tenured captain in command, his platoon was the second biggest. Their symbol was a lightning bolt with an "*x*" at the bottom of it. It stood for hitting hard, fast and accurate. It meant not giving your opponent or enemy a chance to catch you off guard. Daragorn had earned the support and admiration of Drayt and Gilf, and Krum to boot.

Gorga and Stoval were recent advancements to obtain their own platoons. When the second plan to take over Everworld came to fruition, Krum knew he would need more trained captains and more men so he promoted Gorga and Stoval who stood out due to their high levels of intelligence. Gorga's platoon flag played host to a Griffin holding a banner in its claws that read "Ferlaugh!" Ferlaugh is a word in the Centrion language that's equivalent to the English word "devastators" or "devastation". Gorga's nose was the largest of all the Centrion captains, almost to a point of it being out of proportion to the rest of his face. He was of average Centrion height, which was around six and a half feet. Stoval was not much different, although his nose was much smaller. He had very large ears though that protruded much like elephant ears. His platoon's flag held a crescent moon in the middle of a box that was surrounded by a triangle. It was a symbol that stood for keeping an eye on your surroundings and making sure that any cover you had didn't obstruct the ability to see and decipher whatever is around you.

Dragu was the third original captain and Luga the fourth. Dragu was the shortest of the captains. His flag held a picture of an empty, silver helmet with two large horns popping from the crown. It was proof that anyone could lead, even the smaller Centrions. Luga's platoon was led by a banner that hosted the silhouette of a Centrion holding a sword above its head with a circle of stars surrounding it. It served as a memorial of the race that they were fighting for, as Luga was one of the more patriotic of Centrions, and pound for pound he was by far the strongest. All Centrions are fervid about their race. As a whole they are extremely nationalistic, which is why they were such amazing warriors.

Kaen may not have been the tallest or strongest of Centrions but he was by far the nastiest, meanest and most evil Centrion of the entire army. Above and below Kaen's left eye sat a scar. This scar was uneven on each side, being longer underneath and didn't line up properly but that was half due to Kaen's luck of seeing the sword that caused it at the last second and being able to dodge out of the way. That sword belonged to the only Michael Bones to ever visit or be a part of Everworld. The sword that struck Kaen was crafted and bewitched by none other than Azarim. The magic that was cast upon the sword was powerful and left a permanent scar that Kaen could never forget or try to ignore. A scowl lay permanently upon his lips and across his otherwise handsome face – handsome in terms of Centrion beauty. His banner was simple: a black skull upon a dark, red flag. It stood for death; death to his enemies and anyone that stood in his way. Kaen was the first captain under Drayt's, Gilf's, and Krum's leadership.

After looking out across the vast army that was easily twice the size of the previous force that attempted to take over Everworld, Drayt and Gilf turned toward each other. "Remember the plan," Gilf said unquestioningly with a voice that was a tad lighter than Drayt's and sounded more like Earth's Northern Irish in tone. "Everworld will be ours." They turned back to face the sea of Centrions that lay below waiting patiently to hear from their beloved leaders.

The wind was the only cry heard before Drayt spoke up to the crowd: "Friends, brothers, fathers and sons," his voice heavy. "We begin attacks upon the Dark Queen's command. This command shall come within the next couple of weeks. We assume within one week's time our first attack shall be underway." With these words a large cry emerged from the crowd below. Spears and swords alike were thrust into the air with a repetitive pump as cries of war echoed over and over.

"Under the leadership of Krum the Centrions will rule Everworld." Gilf paused before adding, "The Centrions alone will rule Everworld. We will fight alongside Queen Anna, as that has already been planned. However," Gilf spoke this next truth with a commanding voice, "Krum has a new plan that will be put into action near the end when victory is close within our grasp."

Drayt cut back in. "When the taste of victory rests upon our tongues we will turn on the Dark Queen. Her defeat will be quick and our final victory shall be swift. This must remain a secret. Anyone found discussing this will suffer dire consequences."

"When the Dark Queen is destroyed, nothing will stand in our way from ruling all of Everworld," Gilf proclaimed. Another eruption occurred from the crowd as the captains lead their platoons with different chants and howls. "Before the attacks get underway each platoon will be assigned to a specific location of Everworld that they will be in charge of taking over. So, pay attention as these next words will be where you will be deployed to."

"Daragorn and Luga, your platoons will be sent to Undershire. More specifically to Asenfall and Wickamore," Drayt ordered. "Daragorn, your forces will level the southwestern kingdom of Asenfall and destroy the dwarves who inhabit it. Luga, lead your men to the southeast quadrant of Undershire to the fields and forests of Wickamore and conquer those pesky little gnomes." The two captains and their respective platoons let our war cries.

"Dragu and Stoval, your platoons will be sent to Northerntown," Gilf traded off, speaking in place of Drayt. "The Black Forrest Hills and the Valley of Shadows are no cakewalks. Those Natarians are fierce and noble warriors but I have faith that it's nothing you and your men cannot handle. I recommend your platoons work side by side in taking over these two locations. Sweep from the left to right taking out the Natarians last and forcing them back into their valley. Do not allow them to spread out or the task will be even harder."

"That leaves Gorga and Kaen," Drayt stated. Gorga let out his "Ferlaugh" cry while a chorus of "Ferlaugh" echoed out from behind him. Kaen stared silent and menacingly. His cold stare slowly tilted up until it met the eyes of Drayt himself. Without flinching Drayt concluded, "It's up to you and your platoons to take over the large village of Algernon. Once these areas have all been devastated we will band together, surround the central kingdom of Caidel, and attack it from all sides."

There was a restless murmur from the sea of soldiers below that slowly became louder and louder. Drayt and Gilf turned toward each other and squinted their eyes in agreement. They didn't have to say a word to understand what the other thought. It was like they could read each other's mind. It was working, and it would continue to work as long as all went according to plan. They turned back to face the platoons in the valley below for the final time.

"The great culture of the Centrions has struggled for centuries," Drayt started. "We've always been overlooked and under-appreciated. We've been held as slaves and traded like lifeless commodities. The power and intelligence of the Centrion race go much deeper than what appears on the surface. We will win and we will be free from shackles of our past. Everything that has haunted us a culture, and as a race, will vanish and will be destroyed by the entity known as time." Drayt's voice grew louder toward the end of this speech. "Krum won't be back before our attacks. He will be staying at Westershire keeping the Dark Queen occupied and busy while our plans unfold." He ended with this: "Our past will be erased and we will win." Such heartfelt words were only mentally empowering rhetoric. Drayt raised his fist into the air and Gilf copied. War cries thundered out of the valleys below. Everyone was vocally active and morally invested. You could see it in their eyes. Everyone's except Kaen's which held a stinging, beady dullness inside the small sockets.

While the cries of the soldiers came in waves, Drayt and Gilf turned and walked away from the masses smiling devilishly at each other as they did so. Everything was working perfectly.

Chapter 13

BEGINNER'S LUCK

The luckiest people seem to need it the least;
But when luck runs out it gives way to a beast.
From the cradle to the grave you either: have it, don't or lose it.
But one thing is for certain: Don't rely on it or choose it.
If you don't believe in luck, then you've had it all along.
It's just as real as Karma, just as scary, just as strong.

The Magician sat alone in his new room. It was empty except for a bed along the left wall. The bed was neatly made and covered with a couple of sheets and a single pillow lay near its head. The bed he sat upon was such an upgrade from the joke of a bed in his cell that he didn't care. He hoped once he proved himself useful to the Dark Queen that he'd receive room upgrades along with the extra freedoms the queen had promised him. A slit in the wall too small to fit through served as his only window. He walked over to the slit and peered out into the darkness that enveloped the land. He closed his silver eyes and breathed in deep. It had been a long time since fresh air filled his nostrils and lungs. After a brief moment he opened his eyes and stared up into the night sky. He was lucky as not a cloud was covering the sea of stars that twinkled above. The moon's silvery glow matched that of his eyes. He could feel the blood inside his veins begin to thicken and race. He was always stronger at night. Giving himself up to the powers of darkness a long time ago allowed for this strange occurrence. After staring into the night sky for some time he made his way back over to his bed where he stood staring at it thinking of what was to come.

A loose rock along the right wall that seemed to crumble off from pure deterioration caught his attention. He picked it up and examined it, looking for which edge was sharpest and proceeded to etch a circle with that edge in the middle of the floor. The Magician sat down and crossed his legs and placed his hands together in such a formation it almost appeared as if he were praying. The light of the moon trickled in from the slit in the wall and the still air became charged with electricity that swirled around him but suddenly stopped. The Magician furrowed his brows and a look of discontent crossed his lips. His power had weakened considerably while being held hostage inside the dungeon's prison cell. The magic cast upon it prevented him from using his magical abilities. It would take some time before he came back to full power; he just wasn't sure how long. The one thing he did know is that he better get to work fast, regenerating what he could of his powers. The Dark Queen wanted answers and his current condition made the help he promised to provide her with utterly impossible.

A sharp rapping came from the door and the Magician cocked his head to the right and stared out of the corner of his eye.

"Hey, Magician," came Krum's voice. "Come get the pity food the Dark Queen is offering you." Krum placed the plate of food on the floor and slid it against the ground. The Magician looked down upon the bread, potatoes and cheese that sat upon the plate.

"This is not much, but it's more than I got when I was locked down in the dungeon," the Magician muttered to himself. He remembered the queen's promise that once he proved himself worthy and the more he helped her, the more freedoms would come. He stared at the meal before picking it up. "Thank you for the wonderful feast you lay before me," he stated calmly and sarcastically. He began to eat it while Krum gave him a sneer.

"Here's your drink," Krum said. He spilled half of the chalice's contents onto the floor before walking halfway into the room and placing it where the plate had come to a stop. He was so busy he failed to notice the circle the Magician had drawn on the floor. "Have you come up with a name for yourself yet? Her Majesty wants to know what you'd prefer to be called."

The Magician blinked. He'd been so busy figuring out where his powers were at and enjoying his new freedoms that he had forgotten the queen had asked him to do that. "I'll have one soon. Please tell Her Majesty that by the end of the week not only will I be strong enough to help her see past this fog that prevents her, but that I will also have a name for myself. As you may understand I'm not used to having this much freedom."

Krum snorted and walked out of the Magician's new quarters and slammed the door behind him. "Make sure he's not up to something," Krum said. "I want regular checks on him." Both guards nodded before Krum turned away leaving them to their duties.

Back in his room, the Magician finished his meal and wasted no time lollygagging and got back to work honing his powers, which he would do for the next week. He made good on his word not to disobey the queen's orders, for he knew she really would execute him and he had far too much in his future to risk it.

After a week passed the queen requested the Magician's presence. Krum had stayed at Westershire castle that week to keep an eye on the queen in case the Magician decided to come up with the clever idea to disobey her and attack her. It never happened, to their surprise, and the queen's promise of more freedoms also didn't change. The Magician was given more food every day and full drinks along with more bathroom visits and even time outside under the watchful supervision of several Centrion guards.

Krum made his way to the Magician's room and knocked on the door. "Hey, no name," he said in his gruff voice. "The queen demands your presence."

The Magician had been sitting silently with his hands together with a purple aura glowing around him. He kept his eyes closed but opened his mouth to reply. "Actually," he said trying not to laugh, "that's not my new name, but it was a hell of a guess, I'll give you that."

"Well, what is it then?" Krum retorted in a mocking tone.

"That is for Her Majesty to ask." The Magician opened his eyes and stood up. "Oh, please," his sarcasm continuing, "lead the way commander." He outstretched his arm.

Krum narrowed his eyes and grabbed the magician by the collar. "If you continue to mock me I'll destroy you myself once the queen is done with you." The Magician simply smiled and forcefully twitched his legs rapidly inside his boots.

"I'm shaking." His response came with a sly smile.

Krum let the magician go and walked out of the room. The Magician followed behind him as Krum led him down a series of hallways with two guards, one on each side. A few spiders had created webs that now served as decorations along the otherwise bare, stone walls. The torches were nice, but they were so normal and necessary they were just that; more of a necessity than a desired piece of decoration.

The four men came to a large door that the Magician remembered as the queen's quarters. The door stood at least fifteen feet tall and the bolts and latches were made of a sturdy metal that would take a large amount of force to break. Krum knocked on the door and another Centrion guard's voice came from behind it.

"Password?" The voice was deep.

"Password," the Magician mimicked the mystery voice and chuckled.

"Cover his ears!" Krum demanded to the other guards. The Magician made no attempt to block them or fight back. He simply sat there smiling while one of the guards covered his ears. "The password is 'Mally'." Just after he spoke these words the doors unlocked and one slid open giving way to a view of a large room. The guard uncovered the ears of the Magician.

"Go inside and don't try anything funny because I'll be right behind you." Krum stared into the eyes of the Magician with a menacing look.

The Magician bit his lip to prevent himself from saying something and getting himself into trouble. He knew the opportunities this chance would provide him. He entered the room slowly and was greeted by a woman's voice.

"Welcome back to my quarters, Magician. I trust by now your powers are stable enough to help me with what I require?" The queen's eyes never left his. Her raven hair bounced back a white sheen in the moon's rays that blasted into the room.

"Yes, my queen." The Magician bent to one knee and crossed his arm over his chest. He stood back up and bowed.

"Wonderful news," the Dark Queen responded. "Have you chosen a name for yourself?"

"Indeed," he responded.

"Well, go on," her voice seemed to hold a bit of irritation.

"My name shall be Crimson," he stated with no hesitation.

"Crimson," the queen responded in a questioning tone. "May I ask why?"

"You can, but the answer is simple, my queen. I have always enjoyed the way it sounds. I think the word itself is beautiful." The Magician looked past the queen to the blackness that blanketed the outside of Westershire Castle and filled the inside of his heart. His eyes immediately transferred back to hers and he smiled. "But, I dare say you are more than ready to see past the fog that fills your crystal ball. Let us make that fog disappear." His voiced held a more serious tone now.

"Yes," Queen Anna responded as she motioned him over to where her crystal ball sat on the red, velvet pillow. The orb refracted the silver light of the moon that blasted into the room. "Now, watch closely." She swirled her hands around the ball in an attempt to make the image appear, but as soon as the outline of a figure came into focus a slate gray mist filled the ball.

"Is this the fog you speak of, my queen?"

"Correct. Every attempt to make clear the fog just makes it thicker," she explained.

"Allow me, if you will." The Magician sat cross-legged on the ground, placed his hands together and closed his eyes. His body blocked the moonlight from hitting the orb but he absorbed its powers into his back. As he sat silently a purple aura began to glow around him. He opened his eyes to reveal silver irises that seemed to glow as bright as the moon itself inside the dark room. Electricity crackled and flew around him in a fury and a wind seemed to come out of seemingly nowhere. His powers were surely coming back.

"Crimson," the queen said as her eyes grew bigger. This was the first time she had called the Magician by his new name. The wind picked up as she said it and the electricity increased, yet, it wasn't shocking him.

"No need to worry, my queen. I assure you. Please ask Krum to place the pillow and orb upon my lap." Krum did this without the queen needing to ask him. Crimson looked down into the orb and the wind that blew furiously around the Magician seemed to blow the fog away as if they were simply clouds. Both Queen Anna and Crimson looked down as the picture became clearer. A once black outline became a young woman with beautiful blonde hair. Queen Anna's eyes grew large as she clutched the "M" necklace that snuggly hugged her neck.

"That…it's impossible." Her voice was week and her heart began to race. "There's no way in hell," she continued. The image inside the ball circled around the young woman until it reached her face. Queen Anna's heart plummeted for a brief moment and even skipped a few beats after.

"What is it, my queen?" Crimson looked at her. "This traveler has blonde hair. That color hair is not a natural part of this world," he noted and looked up into the lost eyes of the Dark Queen.

"Krum," the queen's voice was so low it was almost a whisper. "Bring her to me at once." Krum bowed and turned around to leave. "Crimson, your services have been incredibly valuable and I thank you for the assistance. Many freedoms will come your way, but I ask that you serve under me still. I think with your abilities and the physical strength of the Centrion Army, taking over Everworld will be an almost effortless challenge." Her focus was still on the girl inside the orb. "Krum," the queen said again, "before you leave to bring her here please take Crimson to his new living quarters and have someone prepare him a hearty meal with plenty to drink. I still require guards at his exit but more time allowed outside his room will be given along with more bathroom visits. Is this understood?"

"As you wish, my queen." Krum bowed and motioned for the magician to stand up. Slowly the wind died down and the purple aura faded as the magician did as he was instructed.

"Thank you, Your Majesty," Crimson stated and bowed to her once more before leaving the queen alone in the moonlit room and following Krum out to his new quarters. A broad smile crossed his face.

They exited the room and made their way through the dimly lit corridors of Westershire Castle. After climbing a few more stairs they came to a room twice the size of the previous room he had before. There was a large window but outside of it was a steep, vertical drop. Floating and hovering were not in the Magician's arsenal of spells, so he knew attempting to leave out the window was impossible. He searched the room and found a large bed with more sheets and larger pillows than his previous one. This was definitely an upgrade and he couldn't help but smile.

"This is your new room, Magician. A meal will be brought up shortly." Krum still didn't trust him.

"Please," said the Magician, "call me Crimson." He brushed some loose hairs behind his ears and a snarky smile played on his face.

"Perhaps," Krum shot back. "You might be gaining the queen's trust but you'll never have mine." Krum's eyes were cold and his fists were clenched by his side.

"Oh, in time I do believe you will change your mind." The smile never left Crimson's face and he chuckled.

Krum left in disgust slamming the door behind him. Crimson laughed and walked over to the window to bask in the light of the moon once more. He looked up at the stars and muttered to himself. "Time is a wonderful, valuable thing." As he finished this sentence he noticed a star glow brightly. Millions of years before that sentence was uttered a star had died and he was staring at a glorious supernova. "Ah," he whispered. "Darkness and light collide once more." The truth of this sentence was far too accurate as the supernova blasted photons through the darkness of space.

Chapter 14

TESTS OF COURAGE AND INTELLECT

Ambushed from all sides
Words of calumny and falsehoods implied
Fight for your dignity
Fight for your pride
Or be swept in darkness where monsters collide

A week had passed since Mallory and Lee were the dinner guests of Annikan Tawah, High Chief of the Valley of Shadows. Now accompanied by Koel Lo'Hota, second in command in the Natarian warrior ranks, they continue their quest to the Silver Lake in the northern most parts of Everworld in search of the Water of Tears. Mallory tried her best to stay hopeful, understanding that every hour, every second, was valuable. With her father's cancer spreading she knew it was a race against the clock.

Back on Earth, Michael Bones did his very best to keep up with Mallory's adventures in Everworld. He couldn't stay awake forever to follow her every step, but he kept the black, hardcover book she was trapped in with him at all times. It stayed on his desk by his bedside when he wasn't reading along. His father in-law, Daniel Frost, Mallory's grandfather, now accompanied him at his house. Since Michael refused to take any notion of the medical advice of any of the doctors regarding chemotherapy, his body kept deteriorating without any chance of recovery. The cancer was spreading fast. Like Mallory, he knew his life was coming to an end, and quickly at that. Daniel promised his son-in-law that he would take care of Mallory until, he too, passed on from old age or whatever might come his way, and at least Michael found some comfort knowing his daughter would be in good hands.

Mallory, Lee and Koel came to a clearing after being surrounded by nothing but trees for what seemed like an eternity, but in reality was only four days. Rushing water could be heard. The sound grew louder as they approached the clearing. What started as the sound of a trickle now sounded more like a cascade and then became a loud roar. A stone cliff came into view which was home to a terrifyingly beautiful waterfall. The dirt path they were on came to an end.

"We're close." Lee's voice could barely be heard over the roar of the waterfall that gushed over the top of the cliff.

"What?" Mallory asked, raising her voice as she tilted her head towards Lee. "Speak up, Lee! I can't hear you!"

"This is Iriss Falls," his voice still low. "Not far beyond this lies Silver Lake." Lee looked at Koel who nodded in agreement.

"What Lee says is absolutely true. The Silver Lake resides no more than a day's hike from here." Koel had been reasonably quiet the last few days. He had been more than happy to answer the random question Mallory had for him. Lee stayed unusually quiet as well. Mallory was unsure of the relationship the Natarians and elves had and figured it best not to ask.

Just then, as Mallory turned to Lee to ask him more about Iriss Falls and why it was named that she saw what looked like a little man with a long, pointy red nose and pointy ears, with long white hair flowing down his back running through the woods. She tried to get a glimpse but the creature had vanished.

"Lee!" she exclaimed. "What was that?" Her voice was full of excitement. She had seen nothing like it up to this point.

"What was what?" Lee had sat down on a rock near the base of the waterfall to rest and refill his canteen with water. He advised Mallory to do the same. Koel had also sat down on a rock not too far away as well.

Mallory started to explain to Lee about the little red man she saw but Koel spoke up before she could go into detail.

"I believe that was a dwarf, though it's hard to be certain. He was moving rather quickly and I only caught a glimpse of him as well."

Lee lifted his head to look at Koel who bent to drink from the base of the waterfall. His eyes squinted in thought as he tied his canteen back to his side. "Are dwarves generally up this far north? I thought they reside in the south in Asenfall?"

"They do," Koel wiped his mouth and bent back up looking into Lee's eyes. "It's incredibly rare to see one this far north. I can only imagine why he was up here."

"And alone at that," Lee responded. "Well, whatever his purpose it didn't seem to regard us. Dwarves are not afraid to come face to face with you if they require something." Lee leaned back on the rock and stretched. Mallory sat too on a large rock and laid back. She stretched out and placed her hands behind her head as she stared up at the sky which was just beginning to darken. The sun would still be out for another three hours or so. It was time to set up camp for the night while they could still see.

Koel took off and unfolded the tents he carried on his back in a bundle. Making shelters every night would have been doable but physically exhausting no matter how good Lee or Koel were at it, so she was incredibly grateful when Annikan explained that he would supply them with extra single shelters for the nights they would spend in the wilds of Everworld.

As night began to fall upon them and the stars began to shine in the indigo skies above, Lee, Koel and Mallory dropped the firewood they had scavenged a half hour before near a circular pit outlined with stones. Lee unbuckled the straps to a pouch on his side and took out some of the food given to them by Annikan. It took a while but after Koel sparked a fire from the kindling they gathered and all three sat around the fire as the yellow-orange flames grew wider and higher.

"Is this all we have left to eat?" Mallory's face expressed an opinion of concern. How were they supposed to finish the journey with such little rations remaining?

"Beginning tomorrow, until this journey is done, we must hunt for our food. Wild forair and even some cloppers reside around the area. I'm used to hunting game such as cloppers and I'm assuming Lee is a fair hunter as well. He is either highly skilled, or his queen is of foul mind sending him off with you on a mission of such importance." His eyes travelled from Mallory's eyes to Lee's face. Mallory could feel an electric tension in the air yet Lee's face remained seemingly unfazed. Sitting cross-legged and stoic, his gaze remained deep within the fire, the flames dancing wildly in his eyes.

"A single shot and almost any forair you want is yours; a promise I'm more than capable of keeping," Lee said in a very calm, yet intimidating tone. His gaze never left the gaseous warmth before them. The electricity in the air died with these words.

"What in Everworld is a forair?" Mallory's forehead grew a bit longer as her eyes contracted in question.

"A moderately sized flying creature," Lee answered swiveling his glance toward Mallory who sat with her knees pulled up to her chin. "In your world I think you call them 'birds'. It's a creature that resembles those except much larger by comparison." Lee ate the remainder of his meal.

"Oh," Mallory responded and followed suit, eating her meal. Once everyone had finished Koel stood up and stretched.

"I'm going to sleep. We have a long journey ahead of us tomorrow if we are to reach the Silver Lake by sundown…" but before the Natarian could finish his sentence the calm, still night became a two-faced liar. Three dwarves jumped down from the tress with shrieks of laughter. Their eyes began to glow in the light of the fire, and their skin, a dark crimson, was tinted an even deeper ruby by the flickering flames. Mallory jumped to her feet in fear but then suddenly became completely immobile. Lee's right hand was already reaching over his shoulder gripping an arrow in his fingertips while his bow sat firmly by his side in his left hand. Koel stood, feet spread, with the right foot slightly in front of the left. An eight inch dagger with a family crest was chest level, the blade parallel to his chest and pointing away from his thumb as he gripped the leather handle tight. His right hand was clenched in a fist by his side.

"Well, well," a deep, screechy voice came from the wide mouth of the dwarf in front of Lee. "An elf and a plains warrior, excuse me, a Natarian, in the same group and no blood has been spilled," he paused, "yet," he finished.

Not yet? Mallory asked herself. Does this mean they are going to attack?

A loud whistle escaped the lips of the same dwarf. Four more dwarves jumped down from the trees.

"What do you want?" Lee's voice was calm and unwavering.

"To challenge your intellect," the dwarf responded. "I'm going to give you a riddle. If you get it right we will leave you in peace. If you get it wrong we kidnap the stranger and kill you. If you try to attack us outright the same event will occur. You know you are good but that you stand no chance against seven of us."

"We don't have time for games!" Koel spat through gritted teeth but Lee raised a hand to silence him.

"Go on," Lee said, "ask your riddle." Mallory stood in silence not knowing what to do. Lee looked over at Koel and smiled with his eyes closed.

"This isn't a game!" the dwarf hissed inching closer. Instead of Lee preparing for a fight he relaxed completely.

"Stay on your guard, Koel," Lee stated and crossed his arms. Koel nodded.

"Lee," Mallory began, wondering why he relaxed. Lee looked at her and shook his head still smiling.

"Lee," the dwarf said. "You must be Lee Odion then."

"And who are you?" Lee responded. "From all the tales on dwarves I've heard, and by that rope wound around your neck that leads to a point in your shirt at your chest, you must be Silverfang." Lee's lip curled as he grinned.

"What is your riddle?" Koel asked. Silverfang scowled at him then stepped back so he could address all three.

"Anyone of you may answer this. It'll probably take all three of you to figure it out anyway with your puny brains," Silverfang chuckled. "Just remember if even one of you says the wrong answer we attack. You're only allowed one answer in total, not individually. He paused for a second, and then began:

Invisible I am to you
You still see me when I show.
I am not fake I'm very real
When my rival loses glow.
Just like the stars that burn out bright
I make it known I'm here.
The greatest hunter in the world
You can't outrun, my dear.
Some may welcome me, some may not
But I will tell you this,
I'm nice enough to free you with a subtle, little kiss."

All was quiet for a minute. Mallory looked to Lee and Koel to see them concentrating on what the answer might be. After a moment Lee smiled. Mallory's heart rose up in her chest.

"Lee, do you have an answer?" Mallory's voice was filled with hope.

"This is not my answer, Silverfang, just a comment before we give our answer," Lee stated.

"Oh, and what is that?"

"You didn't give us a time limit to answer. We could stand here all night thinking if we chose to." Koel grinned along with Lee.

"A dwarf doesn't change a deal once it's accepted," Koel responded.

"Exactly," Lee nodded.

Mallory looked at Silverfang and could swear she saw a quick smile before he spoke.

"Well then, we will wait all night until you answer," Silverfang added with an evil grin.

"We won't need all night," Lee countered.

"You know the answer then? Speak it!" Silverfang demanded.

"Mallory, why don't you answer this?" Lee turned to her and smiled. Mallory, in shock, nodded and brought her hand up to clasp the vial around her neck through her shirt.

"Okay," she thought to herself, "my best shot is to go through the lines one by one." She began:

"*Invisible though I am to you*: Lots of things are visible, yet invisible," she kept monologging in her head. "Things like truth and lies, love, that sort of thing."

"*You still see me when I show.* All of those fit that description as well. Let's keep going."

"*I am not fake, I'm very real.* So, this means it's something that exists or happens."

"*When my rival loses glow.* Whatever it may be it's got a counterpart and this counterpart is bright which means this thing is dark in some sense. That knocks out truth, love or positivity."

"*Just like the stars that burn out bright.* It destroys or at least gets rid of something."

"*I make it known I'm here.* You apparently can't miss this thing. It's a big deal."

"*The greatest hunter in the world.* You can't escape it, then."

"*You can't outrun, my dear.* Same thing," she thought. By this point Koel could almost see the wheels turning inside her head. They spun in his as well. Lee stood smiling motionless just like the windless trees.

"*Some may welcome me, some may not.* That sounds like some sort of personal news. What do some people wish for and others don't? Keep going, Mallory," she told herself.

"*But I will tell you this.* Wait, so can it speak?" Her eyes crossed in confusion. "Well, invisible things can't speak unless they're omniscient or inside your own head. And now lastly…"

"*I'm nice enough to free you with a subtle, little kiss.* Invisible things can't physically kiss, so that's definitely metaphorical. Put it together,

Mallory," she told herself. "It's invisible, yet can be seen. It's dark or possibly evil. It truly exists. You can't escape it, but it can free you with a kiss." She stood there for what felt like an eternity going through the information she had gathered. She turned to Silverfang.

"You have the answer?" Silverfang hissed.

"Before I answer, I want to speak to Lee, please," Mallory finished.

Silverfang looked into her eyes and saw determination. He opened his jaw lined with crooked, pointy teeth and said, "Very well. You are unarmed and he has laid down his weapons. I will give you thirty seconds of communication."

"Thank you!" Mallory exclaimed and walked quickly over to Lee.

"What do you have for an answer?" Lee's voice remained smooth and calm. They spoke to each other in whispers.

"I'm coming up with two possibilities. Is the answer fate?" She looked hopefully into his eyes.

"No, but that's a magnificent guess," Lee said.

"Then is it darkness," she said, worried.

"You are so brilliant, Mallory, for coming up with these answers, but, no," Lee said again.

"Ten seconds!" Silverfang interrupted.

"Lee, I'm so sorry," Mallory said in a panicked voice.

Lee interrupted this time. "It's alright. The answer is death." As soon as the word exited his mouth, Silverfang shouted.

"Time's up! No more speaking! Do you have an answer?"

"We do." Lee was still looking at Mallory whose eyes danced back and forth between Lee's and Silverfang's. "The answer, Silverfang," Lee's voice grew more commanding as his head swiveled and his gaze tilted toward the dwarf, "is death."

Another quick hint of what seemed like a smile crossed Silverfang's face before a scowl stole its place. He stood there silently staring at Lee, Koel and finally Mallory in turn before saying: "Very good. You've solved one of the oldest riddles in Everworld. We'll leave you in peace, as promised." He turned around to leave and the other dwarves followed suit. "We'll see you soon," Silverfang said before turning his head back to the three travelers and chuckling before taking off into the dark woods, his henchman at his rear.

"Time for bed," Koel's voice broke the new silence. "Lee and I will take turns guarding the campsite for the rest of the night. We'll leave at sunrise. The path to Silver Lake from here is a full day's hike."

"He's right," Lee said to Mallory and nodded at Koel, who, surprisingly, nodded back.

"I will take the first watch," Koel said.

While Lee and Mallory changed in their tents Koel found a sturdy stump and propped himself against it as he sat down with his knife in his hands. The silver shine the moon above gave off glinted off the blade of the knife as he turned it over slowly in his hands. He reminisced about the many adventures he had as a boy and the many times this knife had saved his life. It was his grandfather's. The blade was old but the condition Koel kept it in made it appear brand new. He cleaned the blade and handle rigorously and religiously after every use. He remained quiet, listening to the wind ruffling through the trees. The only sound that could be heard was the flaps of the tents closing shut.

Lee kept his bow close by in his tent as he lay upon the soft dirt inside. He didn't want to sleep, but his tired eyes that flickered open and shut were proof enough he needed rest. He still wasn't sure he could fully trust Koel, but if he couldn't now – if Koel let something attack them – he never could. He closed his tired eyes one more time as he drifted off to sleep in a little row boat of hope and trust.

Mallory's mind was racing as she lay down. The day's events swirled in her head like the toilet and its water that she missed and realized she took for granted back on Earth. Her brain fogged over as the events became fuzzy. She was exhausted and found herself blacking out. She'd never been on a journey that was even close to this distance. Mallory took one last deep breath, closed her eyes and almost instantly visited another world called dreamland.

As Mallory's eyes closed in Everworld, Michael's opened back on Earth. He called for Daniel as he sat up in bed leaning against the headrest. Daniel came in through the doorway and sat on the bed next to his dying son-in-law. Michael wiped his eyes with the sleeve of his nightshirt.

"Daniel, how is Mallory?" He stared into Daniel Frost's eyes which gave off a calm reflection of his own face.

"She is fine. No need to worry," he reassured. "If Mallory's life is ever threatened I will wake you right away. Here," he handed the black-covered book with the missing symbol to his son-in-law who thanked him and began to read the events he had missed. "You'll be very proud towards the current end," he spoiled. "I'll go make you some breakfast." He hurried out of the room.

Michael read so fast his eyes could hardly keep up until he reached the dwarf ambush. His heart seemed to thump as fast as his eyes were previously going. He slowed down even more as he read the riddle spoken by Silverfang. Before he read on he thought long and hard about the answer. "Death," he finally whispered before Daniel strode back in holding bacon, eggs and toast on a plate. Daniel placed the breakfast on his lap and saw the lost look in Michael's eyes. "I've heard this riddle somewhere before," Michael said.

"That's strange," said Daniel. "Oh well, finish reading to the current point. She should have just fallen asleep."

Michael finished reading but before he reached the dwarves exiting the campsite a broad smile had crossed his face. Mallory sure was a smart cookie. He was so proud of the intelligent young woman she had become. He internally thanked both Lee and Koel for having the right answer and staying on guard for his daughter's life respectively.

He closed the book and tried handing it back to Daniel who refused. "Right now I must admit I need my own rest," Daniel said with a smile and a slight yawn.

"Of course," said Michael. "Sleep well." Daniel made his way out of the room as Michael began to eat his breakfast. One single thought couldn't escape him. "Where have I heard that riddle before?" And then, it clicked.

Chapter 15

TESTS OF INTELLECT AND VALOR

Questions, not answers,
Still have a correct ending
Answer if you dare

Sunlight bounced off the tent that sheltered Mallory from Everworld's natural elements. Her eyes opened leading to a long yawn and a stretch of her limbs. Small sounds of rustling could be heard outside her tent. She dressed back into her clothes and unzipped the front flap. Lee was walking around cleaning up their campsite as Mallory approached.

"Good morning, Mallory," came Lee's voice before Mallory could even open her lips. He turned to look at her.

"Good morning, Lee. I'm assuming Koel is sleeping. During the night while I slept you two changed guard. I remember you telling me that."

"Yes. Yesterday was quite an eventful day. Hopefully you slept well. Today is the day we reach the Silver Lake. I'll be waking Koel up shortly and once we have everything packed we will begin our journey."

"What about breakfast?" Mallory asked.

"Oh," Lee stated. "Right, I forgot about that. Elves don't eat as much. Our biological systems break down food slower than other races giving us an advantage during long bouts on the battlefields. We shall eat breakfast then proceed to begin the last leg of our journey to the lake. But, remember what I told you. Fairies guard the Silver Lake. You must be ready to face the challenge they lay for you or else you will be denied access to the Water of Tears."

"What exactly are these tasks?" Mallory asked.

"The can range in variety. There is no simple answer to your question, Mallory Bones."

Just then, Koel came out of the tent provided by Lee earlier in the night as he had kept watch. He nodded to both Lee and Mallory as he began to pack it up. After it was packed he turned to Lee. "I know elves don't eat as much as other races but Mallory and I should have a small meal before heading out. We will need the energy for later when we reach the Lake"

"Yes," replied Lee. "That is something Mallory and I had just discussed before you awoke."

Koel nodded and turned to Mallory. "What are you thinking you want?" Mallory smiled.

As breakfast came to an end and everything was packed it was off to the races again as they made their way through the Black Forrest Hills. The density of the forest began to lessen as they approached the most northern area Everworld had to offer. The once bright skies began to gray, but the clouds weren't rolling in. They were rolling towards the clouds that seemed to sit still like a puppet on a shelf. The last of the trees gave way to a misty area that was undeniably the home of Silver Lake. A small flock of child-sized fairies came floating out of the mist. Their large, colorful wings swirled up to points. They wore nothing yet seemed not to be naked. About ten fairies in total, male and female, hovered in front of the three travelers who happened upon their place of residence.

Mallory's eyes lit up. She had read about fairies, but they were fictional, mystical creatures, yet, here they were, in the flesh. Then she remembered she was magically transported into a book that, unbeknownst to her, magically added text with every move she made and every obstacle she had to overcome. Suddenly, the magic didn't seem all that magical or fictional anymore for that matter. Still, seeing real fairies for the first time made her awestruck. Both Koel and Lee bent down on one knee, Lee pulling Mallory down with him, heads bowed.

"We've come to talk to the Elder-Ones," Lee said in a light tone. Mallory had never heard him talk this way before. It was like there was fear in his voice.

"Why have you come? What is your purpose, Elf of Algernon?" One of the female fairies said as she circled around them.

"This traveler that kneels beside me is not part of this world," Lee said before he was cut off.

"That is prudently evident," the female fairy interrupted as she tilted up Mallory's head and stared into her eyes. "Such confusion, discomfort and loss drown your eyes. Why is that, strange traveler?"

Mallory looked over at Lee who motioned for her to reply. "I came here to this world by mistake. I was transported here after removing a symbol from a book…"

"We understand this," a male fairy with blue hair and blue around his eyes said impatiently. "What is your purpose for coming to the Silver Lake?"

"My father," Mallory started but the words caught in her throat which dried up like a desert.

"What about your father?" the male fairy continued in a silvery voice.

"Please," Koel said with his head still bowed. "If you will, please allow me to explain to save this girl from the heartache of which she's come here."

"Proceed," said the female fairy that had circled them upon arrival.

"This is Mallory Bones," Koel began. Some of the fairies whispered to each other before the male fairy motioned them silence. "Mallory has come to ask permission to challenge for a small amount of the Water of Tears. Her father lay dying in her world with the Final Death. She wishes to obtain a small amount of the Water of Tears to heal him and save him from death."

"The Water of Tears is carefully, closely and strongly guarded by the Elder-Ones," the female fairy spoke again. "The water must not be overused. If everyone came to use it its supply would run dry and there would be no way to replenish it. It would cease to exist. The only time the Water of Tears may be obtained is in dire situations. However, in this situation, we allow you to speak to the Elder-Ones."

"Thank you very much," Mallory bent even farther down.

"Understand this, Mallory Bones, you may be allowed to challenge for the Water of Tears but unless the challenge is complete, you will obtain none. Before the challenge is submitted by the Elder-Ones, they must approve of the situation. Do you understand this? There is a possibility that you may not even be allowed to challenge."

"Yes, I understand," Mallory replied looking up into the eyes of the fairy that spoke this harsh reality to her.

"Then rise, lay down your weapons and follow us to the lake." She motioned to all the fairies – except the male who spoke to them earlier – to go back and alert the Elder-Ones of their arrival. "My name is Arovia, Mallory Bones."

"And my name is Arra," the male fairy spoke as the two fairies led the trio to the lake where the Elder-Ones awaited their arrival.

Four fairies – two male and two female – floated near the closest border of the lake to Mallory, Lee and Koel. They looked young, these Elder-Ones, but by no means were they. Their faces still held smooth curves and their skin looked soft as silk. The Elder-Ones were slightly larger than the other fairies who resided in Silver Lake, except for a female with a purple aura who was still small enough to fit into two hands. This fairy floated in front of Mallory's face, her small eyes staring into Mallory's. Lee and Koel dropped to a knee while Mallory lifted her left hand up into a cup formation. She did this without thinking. Lee tried to motion her to bow but Mallory never saw him signaling. The fairy circled her head and came back into view floating a foot from her face.

"Child, there is so much sadness in your eyes. You're not from this world." These words were spoken as the fairy landed softly into the cupped hand of Mallory Bones. The Elder-Ones watched closely as the next series of events unfolded. Mallory raised her cupped hand back to eye level. "My name is Lilia; I am the oldest of the Elder-Ones. What brings you to the Silver Lake? Those who make the journey come with reason, or else are a fool."

Mallory waited a few seconds to make sure Lilia had finished speaking. "I am from a place called Earth. Back in my home world, my father is dying of a disease called cancer. It is the same disease known here as the Final Death. I come to the Silver Lake to ask for a challenge in order to receive a vial of the Water of Tears, so that when I get home I can cure him of his disease and grow up with him by my side. I don't want to lose my father. I have already lost my mother." Mallory's eyes started to swell and clear, salty liquid lined her lower eyelids. Her head tilted forward as a single tear fell from Mallory's right eye like a fat raindrop onto her wrist. A small splash landed on Lilia.

"Child, lift your chin up. Some things in life we can control, and others we cannot. You'll find in life that both seemingly fair and unfair happenings will be a part of your life. This is the natural order of things. Most of the time we turn away those seeking the water for cheating death because death is a natural part of life, however, I will go and speak to the other elders and we will determine whether we find the matter suitable. Do not take those as harsh words, young one. Every situation becomes discussed but I cannot promise a certain outcome until every elder has heard and had a chance to be heard." With this final line, Lilia levitated off Mallory's hand. Mallory's gaze rose until it met the eyes of the Elder-Ones fairy once more. Mallory wiped the tear from her eyes and nodded. Lilia turned away and began to fly back to the other three Elder-Ones.

"Elder Lilia," Mallory spoke. She was unsure of what to call her. She wasn't accustomed to addressing fairies, especially those in power. Lilia stopped flying and floated in the air. Before she could turn around, Mallory finished, "I'm sorry, I'm not sure how to address a fairy in power like yourself, please excuse any rudeness. I simply want to say 'thank you'. Thank you for even taking the time to listen to me. Your words will rest in stone in my heart forever." Mallory kept her head up. Lilia never turned around.

"You're welcome, Mallory Bones. We shall be back shortly with an answer for your challenge request." Lilia flew off back to the group of Elder-Ones.

When Lilia approached the group floating near the edge of the lake the four Elder-Ones flew in a group from the edge of the lake and over to the middle of it where they sat in a cloud of mist and began to discuss the situation.

Lilia began: "Did all of us hear what young Mallory Bones had to say?"

"She is clearly not from our world. The only way she could find out about the Water of Tears is through the Queen of Algernon. This isn't taking anything away from Mallory, but what would she have done if she never ended up in our world? She could lose her father with or without the Water of Tears." These words came from the other female Elder-One who had an aura of red wrapped around her like a bubble. She was the shortest of the Elder-Ones and also the youngest.

"Yes," a male fairy with a light blue aura chimed in. "She is lucky to have stumbled upon a cure for her dying father. The poor young girl has lost both her mother and soon to be her father depending on our decision."

"What Evoron says is true," came from the last Elder-One. "But let us add in a hiding factor to this colloquy. This girl, very young and very inexperienced to the world, somehow came to this world and, while yes, was helped out by leaders of trustworthy races, she still fought against the unknown and their odds. She could very easily have been killed and who's to say she won't be if we do decide her situation deems important enough."

"But, how can we be sure if she is telling us the truth? Who's to say she isn't going to use the water for acts with evil intentions. We don't even know much about this Earth of which she speaks except for the one other human who came here a long time ago, and we did not even associate with him. We were told about him by Queen Evana."

"Nixa, you make an intelligent an understandable point." Lilia looked at both Evoron and Taroa. Both nodded their heads in agreement. "However," continued the oldest Elder-One, "we cannot just simply cast aside her opportunity."

"She does this for the sake of someone else and she is accompanied by the right-hand man of Queen Evana. There is no doubt Lee has had extensive training in identifying someone with undesirable intentions," Evoron pointed out.

"Indeed," agreed Taroa."

Lilia swiveled her head amongst the other three fairies. "So, we must take a vote to decide if Mallory Bones deserves an opportunity. The vote must be unanimous."

"I am for Mallory Bones being given an opportunity to challenge," Taroa voted.

"I join Taroa in that regard," Evoron noted.

"What say you, Nixa?" Lilia waited patiently for an answer as Nixa thought.

"What will be her challenge?" asked Nixa. "I am not against her receiving an opportunity but before I cast my vote I reserve the right as an Elder-One to ensure the highest possible safety of the Silver Lake's Water of Tears." Lilia smiled at this. Nixa had been the newest addition within the last century to the Elder-Ones after the previous had eventually passed of old age. As she was welcomed into the new position she paid the utmost attention when learning what she had to know and her duties as an Elder-One. She had come a long way very quickly. It was something to be proud of.

"Her challenge will be a riddle. To be more specific, the most difficult riddle in all of Everworld. I know this challenge may seem a bit too easy but I need your trust that this one specifically is not. It relies on an immense amount of intellect and valor along with trusting one's self. I believe this will show us if Mallory truly deserves a vial of the Water of Tears."

Nixa thought for a little hovering in the silent air. "It's impossible to tell without giving her a chance I suppose." She gave a brief pause. "Alright, I accept giving Mallory an opportunity for the water."

Lilia nodded. "So it's unanimous. Mallory Bones has been granted permission to challenge for the water."

"It appears so," Evoron said. All nodded and all flew back to the lake's edge.

Purple aura aglow, Lilia approached Koel and Lee who were still kneeling with their heads bowed.

"Elf of Algernon, Valley Warrior, please state your name and rank."

Lee spoke first. "I am Lee Odion, head warrior of the elven race and right-hand man of Queen Evana."

"I am Koel Lo'Hota, second in command of the proud Natarian warriors."

"Elf warrior of Algernon and tribal warrior of the Valley of Shadows, we have granted Mallory Bones of Earth an opportunity to challenge for a small portion, or more specifically, a vial full, of the Water of Tears. Please rise," Lilia insisted. They did. She continued: "Your ranks indicate on the surface that you've been briefed on what the Water of Tears is and what its powers are. Does this hold true?"

Koel and Lee looked at each other then turned back to face Lilia. Standing erect and with their hands clenched into fists by their side they nodded and bowed quickly and respectfully.

"Very well, you also know then that it has possible unknown capabilities. It is an immensely powerful substance; the most power-ful in all of Everworld. If Mallory does complete the challenge and gains possession of the water, the two of you will be responsible for her safety and for the security of the water. Do you understand this?"

As if they shared vocal chords, both spoke at once: "Yes, Elder-One."

"Very well," Lilia said and then flew to where Mallory was standing. "Are you ready for your challenge?"

Mallory stood silent for a brief moment with thoughts of her past shooting through her mind up to the present exploding like fireworks. She thought of her father who lay slowly dying back on Earth and, who, unbeknownst to her, read along as her journey unfolded. "I am ready, Elder-One," she proclaimed.

"Then listen closely here my child. Your challenge will be to solve a riddle."

"Another riddle?" thought Mallory. "What is it with this world and riddles?"

"Koel Lo'Hota and Lee Odion may not help or interfere in any way or else you fail the challenge by default."

"Lee, Koel, please turn away. I need all temptations of help gone." They did as Mallory instructed.

"Intelligent move, now…"

Mallory tensed up. Everything rode on her answer – one shot. Lilia began:

"The answer to this riddle is the answer to this riddle

    It is nothing more, nothing less, if you think too hard you'll never guess

    It is at the front and at the end, a helping hand no one can send

    Everything will not be right, yet nothing makes you lose the fight

    As you dissect this poem by whittle you'll find the answer to this riddle"

Koel and Lee stood in silence. Neither had heard this riddle before and both minds raced for an answer.

"Elder-One, Lilia," Mallory asked, "how much time do I have to guess?"

"As much as needed," Lilia countered.

"Thank you. My next words will be my answer," Mallory promised.

"As you wish."

Mallory broke the poems down in segments with each line being its own segment – just as she did with her previous run-in with the dwarves. In her head she began:

The answer to this riddle is the answer to this riddle. What kind of line is that? Of course it is! This doesn't help at all, at least yet anyways.

It is nothing more, nothing less. Again this seems unhelpful at the moment.

If you think too hard you'll never guess. Finally, this is something I can work with! This means don't dig too deep into this or you may just be wrong.

It's at the front and at the end. Let's hold unto this until I reach the end then.

A helping hand no one can send. I must do this on my own. I can't receive help. That was made obvious even before this poem. What is Lilia trying to get at?

Everything will not be right, yet nothing makes you lose the fight. If everything is not right how can there be an answer? Yet, there must be something because if I say nothing I also lose the fight which I assume means the challenge. I lose the fight to save my father.

Let's finish: *As you dissect this poem by whittle, you'll find the answer to this riddle.* So, as I break this riddle down I'll find the answer. In other words I must carve it down to the root. Okay, take your time Mallory and think, she said to herself.

As Mallory stood in silence like Koel and Lee, back on Earth Michael Bones dissected the poem himself. He lay in bed silently as the words paused their birth on the pages. About half an hour went by; over and over the lines went in his head. He started to laugh. His laughs grew loud enough to make Daniel come stumbling in.

"Michael," he gasped.

"I'm fine, Daniel," Michael said with a cough and a final chuckle. "Do you remember the first time Morgana and I fought?"

"Yes. We were all so much younger. It was a rainy day and you and Morgana had different ideas about how to spend it. You wanted to go to the movies but Morgana wanted to stay home."

"She was sixteen years old and I was seventeen. We were high school sweethearts. We stood in your kitchen arguing about why. It escalated and she yelled at me to leave. She ran upstairs and locked her door."

"Yes," Daniel agreed, "her first real heartbreaking fight."

Michael coughed a couple of times. "I put my coat on to leave and you gently grasped me by the elbow as I reached for the door. It scared the hell out of me. I thought my ass was toast."

"Is that what I smelt?" Both started laughing and Michael coughed again.

"Do you remember what you told me?" Michael looked into the sullen eyes of Daniel Frost. "You said: 'Son, I'm not upset. There's something I want to tell you.' You released my elbow and I turned to face you. You asked: 'Do you know why she's so upset?' I said: 'No sir. Is it because I didn't do what she wanted?' You replied: 'That's close, but no.' I said: 'I just don't understand why she made it so com-plicated.' You replied: 'Do you know why people complicate things?' I shook my head." Michael coughed again. "You said: 'People are afraid of and don't understand simplicity. They believe everything needs a rhyme or reason. The truth is sometimes life's hardest ques-tions have the simplest of answers.' I'll never forget that. You finished with: 'She doesn't have a reason. She simply just didn't want to go, nothing more, nothing less." Michael smiled and grabbed Daniel's hand. "Thank you," he choked. Daniel sat confused for a while then smiled back. Michael looked at the silent book and whispered, "Oh, Mallory, my sweet, sweet girl. Don't fear simplicity, and don't fear failure. I'll always be proud of you no matter the outcome." He leaned back smiling and closed his eyes. "The answer to the riddle is the answer to the riddle."

"No," Mallory thought, "that can't be right because everything will be wrong." She took a deep breath and exhaled. As she did so a light breath of wind stirred the silence and tickled her ear.

"Don't fear simplicity. Don't fear failure." A soft whisper of a disembodied voice filled her ears.

What the…? she thought before the voice whispered only once more.

"The answer to the riddle is the answer to the riddle."

She quickly rehearsed the riddle in her head and thought again of what the voice said. "Don't fear simplicity. Don't fear failure." Her eyes snapped open and quickly traveled to Lilia expecting to hear her say in some way that she had received help and that she failed. However, Lilia floated silently until their eyes connected. Mallory's heart was racing so fast it could beat a cheetah in a footrace.

Lilia's lips parted as words escaped them, "Mallory, do you have an answer?"

Mallory's heart skipped a beat. How could Lilia not have heard the voice? Did anyone except herself hear it? She slowed her pulse with deep breaths. She didn't know how it happened and she didn't care at this point. Deep down she knew this was her only shot and it came from a disembodied voice. She thought the words once more. "Don't fear simplicity. Don't fear failure." She nodded. Koel and Lee's hearts grew cold in fear. "The answer to this riddle," - their biological thermometers fell even lower – "is the answer to this riddle." The hearts of the elven and Natarian warrior froze solid.

Lilia floated in silence again for a short period that felt like an eternity. She smiled. "Your father seems to have taught you well. You have come a long way to get here. You've faced the unknown in a world you know nothing of in hopes to help your father. He has indeed taught you well," she paused before adding, "And you have successfully completed the challenge."

The frozen hearts shattered into crystal fragments leaving the warmth of Mallory's smile to melt them away. "Thank you." It's all that her lips could let loose. Lilia nodded and floated back to the Elder-Ones. Koel and Lee turned around, Lee smiling and Koel too stunned to express any emotion besides shock. They walked up to Mallory who was beaming blissfully.

When Lilia reached the Elder-Ones she informed them of Mallory completing the challenge successfully.

"It truly is amazing that such a young girl was able to understand the importance and complexity of simplicity," Taroa said.

"Agreed," exclaimed Evoron. "She has earned a right to access the Water of Tears."

"As much as I fear what may come of this, her opportunity has been earned," Nixa stated.

"We are all on the same page," noted Lilia. "Mallory, please approach the lake and open the vial that hangs around your neck." Mallory did what was asked of her. "Please hand it to me."

Mallory handed the vile over to Lilia who proceeded to fill it with the Water of Tears. The silver, almost translucent liquid slid down the vial's tubing. It seemed thicker than normal water but not by much. It acted as though it was very thin syrup. Lilia handed the vial back to Mallory who clasped it back behind her neck and slid it underneath her shirt. This element from another world that was the only chance of saving her father's life rested upon her heart.

"On behalf of the Elder-Ones and all the fairies of Everworld we wish you luck, Mallory Bones." Lilia nodded as did the other Elders as they floated back toward the center of the lake disappearing trough the mist like melting snow.

"Well, let's go!" Mallory said with more enthusiasm than ever before.

Koel's shock had left his body and he smiled. "Let us get you home, Mallory. I believe your father misses you terribly."

They turned around and headed back south. After a few hours they reached an area past the point where they had their encounter with the dwarves. There were no dwarves this time but heavy footsteps could be heard only a few yards out. It was hard to tell with the fog rolling in, the day turning into night and the Black Forrest being naturally dark.

A large figure with a boar's head appeared out of the fog. Koel and Lee were knocked unconscious from behind. The soft dirt of the forest masked the footsteps of the enemy.

"Hello, my name is Krum, and you will come with me." Mallory's scream echoed through the Dark Forrest only to be left mostly unheard.

Chapter 16

THE CAPITAL, THE PRINCE AND THE OLD MAN

When friendly faces reappear
The hope that rises drowns the fear
An army of dark that tries to rise
Will find a fight to their surprise

Covered in a tattered, old brown cloak, a man with a staff in his left hand hobbled up to the big wooden door that kept the cold air out of Caidel Castle. He used the staff as a crutch that helped his old body move along the cobblestone pathway leading up to the entrance. His long white beard and long gray hair matched each other's endpoints which just happened to be the hips of the traveler. His hand, rather generous in strength for his apparent age knocked firmly on the door. A guard encased in a chain link suit of armor answered the call.

"Please go away beggar. Our prince is very busy at the moment. Leave your name and state your business. If it's money you desire the prince would rather buy you a house than risk you spending given money on booze or other wasteful desires," the guard said before continuing. "He wishes to see no one homeless but refuses to help feed an unhealthy addiction."

"Your prince is very kind indeed." The words came from the voice of the old man. "But it is not money, food or an abode that I desire. I must speak to your prince at once. Please inform him that Zarim wishes to speak solely to him. I ask this one request. If I'm rejected I will leave without a fuss."

The young guard clad in chain link looked closely at the old man. "I will do as you ask but you must wait out here."

"Very fine," the old man stated. The guard closed the door and the old man sat down upon the steps that led up to the Castle door.

The guard rapped upon the prince's door and the prince answered as quickly as he could. The door opened and in the doorway stood a man, human in form. He was above-average height, six-foot-eight, and his hair was dark, raven black like his big almond eyes. He stood for a moment before addressing the guard.

"What is it Ishmael? Is all okay?"

Ishmael bowed and spoke: "There is a man at the main door who appears to be a beggar. I told him that you would help him find new shelter, but he insisted that was not what he came here for. He stated he would leave, but only after I told you that Zarim wishes to speak solely to you."

The prince's already big eyes expanded even further as he nodded and said, "I will go to the door personally and talk to this beggar." The guard opened his mouth to protest but the prince continued:

"Fear not, Ishmael. For I know this man. He is an old friend." The guard moved aside as the prince made his way down the steps from his chambers to the front door. He opened the door to find the old man in the tattered cloak sitting on the steps facing the capital city of Caidel, the centerpiece of Everworld.

The old man stared away from the castle as the prince looked at him for a minute then sat beside him upon the stone steps.

"It's a beautiful place," said the old man, "for a city that is."

The prince chuckled and agreed. "I do my best." The prince looked over at the old man and he returned the glance, both smiled. "You have returned, Zarim. I had believed I would never set eyes upon you again. I'm jubilant to see you." He looked down upon the staff that Azarim used as a cane. "I wish I could say in better health."

Azarim raised his hand and spoke, "I am old. Body's age and spirits pass. I'm grateful and overjoyed to see you again too, old friend." Azarim rose and the prince followed. "The stars have aligned in a very mischievous pattern and my old bones have begun to ache. I fear a winter of discontent is upon us."

"What do you mean?" the prince asked.

"I have reason to believe that the Centrion Army has been building for quite some time. Queen Anna seems to be behind the uprising. It is no surprise seeing as her predecessor, mentor and friend Evelyn, wished for the same desire. Your rule over Everworld is threatened, Prince Alderous. Everything your family has worked for to make this a wonderful world is on the verge of collapse. The Centrion Army has more than doubled in size. The Humanus Army of Caidel is strong, but no match for the new Centrion Army on its own."

"We must find out the validity of this belief and if it's proven to be true we must ask the elvish and Natarian warriors for assistance. We may even have to ask the dwarves for help. The gnomes are too proud and carefree a race to care. They will go on thriving either way."

"Alder," Azarim hesitated, "I also have reason to believe there is an outsider in our world." Azarim called him his shortened name out of affection for his old friend. The prince preferred this to his full name.

"An outsider," Alder's eyes thinned as he thought. "Has Michael Bones returned to Everworld?"

"It may be so, but I believe this to not be the case. This outsider is new to this world. I have had no chance to find out who they may be or what their desire is. We must remember Queen Anna is an outsider as well."

The prince nodded reassuringly. "We must send spies out to the Muddy Hills region to confirm or expel this belief. All of Everworld depends on the findings."

Azarim walked up the stairs, staff in hand, until he reached the base of Caidel Castle and looked out upon the landscape that was covered in a sheet of dark gray. Night was falling upon Caidel and tomorrow Prince Alder would send his spies.

"What is it Azarim?"

"Nothing," said Azarim. "Would you mind if I stayed with you until knowledge of the situation has presented itself? Your life is important and I would not risk the possibility of your capture."

"Stay as long as you wish. I will have the maids prepare a room for you and food brought to you by our chefs."

"I can find my way to the dining hall. I'm not that old," Azarim chuckled, "not yet!"

The prince smiled and both turned to look out upon the land-scape. Shops and villages turned out their lights for the night. The now quiet city began to sleep. A half-moon had begun rising a few hours prior and hung high overhead in the vast blackness of space. Stars began to appear as the final oranges and blues fell from the sky. Azarim lit the end of his wooden staff with a flame that helped guide them inside. Azarim took one last look behind him as the doors shut for the night on Caidel Castle. Trouble was coming. He could feel it in his old, weary bones.

Chapter 17

ASENFALL FALLS

Smaller doesn't always mean weaker
Big hearts sometimes lay in small chest
Taller doesn't always mean stronger
They can topple and fall like the rest
But sometimes the numbers may win
And sometimes the fewer may lose
But laying down a forfeit is sin
When a right to live is what you can choose

The blazing orange fields complimented the blue sky that carried a blazing orange sun. The sun that gave warmth and light to Everworld was setting, giving way to the same stars that Crimson looked out upon a couple of days prior. The sky was painted with a majestic pastel of fall colors which was common in Undershire. While this beautiful sight unfolded, a more sinister, ugly picture came to rest upon the rolling hills that would soon be set ablaze.

Daragorn and his platoon of Centrions halted at the same time that Luga's did. They looked down upon the hills they wished to conquer in the name of the Centrions with a false promise to Queen Morgana. With his fist held high in the air it would be a matter of seconds until carnage reigned rampant. They looked down upon a village of stone homes that would soon be turned to rubble with a small gleam in their beady black eyes.

A dwarf about the same size as Silverfang appeared to pop out the far-side on one of the many hills that littered Asenfall. He was on his way to a tree that stood at the base of a hill which he occupied. Unaware of the Centrions that would invade at any moment he picked a small purple fruit in the shape of a trapezoid from beneath silver leaves from the tree. He gathered himself and continued onward scuffling back to the village he and the majority of other dwarves called home.

Daragorn's fist dropped like a judge's gavel hitting its block, and Luga's followed. They both bellowed a mighty roar as the Centrions stormed down the hill like a stampede of bulls. Daragorn and Luga felt the wind whip past them as their soldiers sped down the hills. After the final soldier of each platoon ran past their respected officers, the officers themselves joined in on the destruction and fall of Asenfall.

The dwarf who had been unaware of the darkness headed his way turned in horror as he saw a sea of half-humanoid, half-boarish bodied creatures with the head of bulls flying down the hill. The sound was thunderous. His heart began to pound hard and heavy. He dropped his recently picked fruit in a panic and began sprinting towards the village homes he was simply meandering towards before the monstrosity began. He tried to scream to attract the attention of the villagers but out of extreme fear his words caught in his now dry mouth. He saw it was pointless to scream anyways because the thunder that blundered down the hills caught the attention of the other inhabitants of Asenfall.

Screams of surprise and fright echoed throughout the hills which in turn led to more dwarves appearing from their homes to see the cause of the commotion. On and on this progression went until the entire village became aware of the horror unfolding. The Dwarven Army gathered in a mass to fight off the onslaught of Centrions but the numbers were far too lop-sided for the army alone to have a chance at staving off the enemy. It became apparent to the other dwarves what needed to happen in this dire situation. Finding anything they could swing, throw or joust they joined the Dwarven Army for the battle of their lives. Both men and women dwarves gathered the children and hurried as many of them as possible to the outer village in a retreat to Wickamore. The gnomes there were tricky and vicious, but trying to reason with them was better than this. This was the hope of those fleeing to protect the lives of not only their bloodline future but the future of the entire race.

A Centrion with a gigantic nose bashed in a wooden door to one of the stone houses. He knocked over a pot of still burning coals which created a small fire that rose in size as it engulfed the inside of the previously peaceful home. The stone home would contain most of the fire but with the door now broken away, sparks were free to fly out into the orange grass. The colors blended and it became impossible to tell grass from fire until the flames rose high into the sky. A recent dry spell created an easy spread as the tiny fire became a river of flames. A sea of flames was soon to come.

Dark, heavy gray smoke rose into the sky, turning a bright, dry day into a volcanic, ashy night. Choked screams from gassed dwarves popped erratically like bubbles brewing in a cauldron. The Centrions, from the shadowed muddy hills of western Everworld, were more acclimated to the affect as volcanoes were a common sight standing alongside mountains of dead trees.

Roars continued to bellow. One after another, dwarves continued to fall as heavy thunking sounds could be heard from clubs and axes that penetrated their red-skinned bodies. White hair became red as splatters of blood flew like raindrops from the gray clouds of smoke above. The roars weren't only cries of victory but those of pain as the dwarves fought back. Their sharp teeth and swords forged by their greatest blacksmiths cut deep into the tough skin of the Centrions. A small dwarven warrior named Ferlone toppled a few of the invading Centrions before retreating to get a better view of the battle and catch his breath before jumping back into battle. Other dwarf soldiers held their own for long periods but the Centrion numbers were far too great. With the fear and desire to live, the hearts of the dwarves made the battleground a more even match, but the odds were stacked against them.

Luga made his way, slicing and gashing as he went with a smile on his face and his mouth agape as he laughed. He came upon a rather large dwarf who was fighting a rather small Centrion when Luga plunged his sword through the back and heart of one of the dwarven generals named Poco. Luga turned away and rampaged his way through the ashy air to find Daragorn. Poco let out a small gasp and cry as he fell to the ground. Ferlone, who had rushed back into battle, saw the general fall and cried out to him. He kneeled beside Poco as the fallen general lay bleeding. His white hair now coated in a red blood matched that of his garments. The hole created by Luga's sword was far too big to heal. Poco pulled Ferlone closer, his clawed hands gripping his neck garments, spoke a single word before he fell into everlasting darkness: "Caidel."

Chapter 18

WICKAMORE WONDERS

A thousand bulls, a hundred men
Numbers tumble by battle's end
When nobody wins, they all will lose
Both tribes, now weak, sing solemn blues

Wickamore, a lot like Asenfall, was generally a peaceful home to a cunning and conniving race. Wickamore was the abode to the gnomes of Everworld. These creatures weren't evil but they were very protective of their home and loved to play witty, practical jokes on those they happened to cross, or those who happened to cross paths with them. The dark green grass also lay upon rolling hills except there were many more trees; so many trees it was like a jungle had appeared out of nowhere. The gnomes called these trees home, while many more called the undergrounds home. The roots of the giant, dense trees created a wonderful roof to the underground homes.

Now that Asenfall had fallen and while smoke still hung high in the sky, the Centrion warriors made their way across the southern borders of Undershire and the northern borders of the Capecian Sea. Daragorn and Luga were tired and sporting wounds along with the rest of the Centrion legions that served under them. A day's rest wouldn't heal the broken warriors' bodies but would heal their spirits which was exactly the opposite of what the unaware gnomes whished for. They staggered their way, dragging their weapons and stumbling over their own feet to the outer edges of Wickamore. A large mass of boulders outlined the jungle-like forest. The legions took rest behind the boulders to hide from sight. Warriors from each platoon took shifts watching over and making sure their presence was still unknown as night came. A small glow of red fire still blazed off in the distance. It would be years before Asenfall would rebuild, under the regime of the Centrions or otherwise. The darkness of night would take over as the far-off fire burned slowly to ash. The clouds of smoke that had drifted across the southern borders had begun to evaporate and a cold breeze began to rifle through. The thick, hairy bodies of the Centrions would keep them nice and warm as their cold-hearted ambitions carried them through.

Blue skies began to appear. The Centrions were waking up one by one as the sun began to rise into the navy blue sky. The sun added a mixture of white which tainted the blue to a much lighter variant as the morning progressed. The warriors gathered around their respective generals and listened to the instructions of today's agenda.

"Good morning wimps," Daragorn said in a haughty manner.

"Good morning fairies," Luga addressed his platoon. The Centrions groaned and mumbled at the disgust of being compared to those little pests from the north. Instructions began as the platoons listened carefully. It was a challenge keeping the booming voice low enough as to not be heard by the gnomes. The Centrions grinned in a surreptitious manner and nodded understandingly. The clump of warriors dispersed as their platoon lines reformed and the marching commenced again as they appeared from behind the boulders and headed deep into the shadows that would cost them more lives than they were prepared for.

The dense trees created an eerie setting which perfectly complemented the dirty deeds that were underway. It was impossible to keep quiet in the woods as twigs and branches snapped under the heavy footfalls of the Centrions. Daragorn and Luga lead their troops deeper and deeper in. The once blue sky overhead became forest green with peeks of sunshine bleeding through the cracks in the overhead branches. Even the sunlight refused to show after a short while. The forest green became a dark green sliding slowly into a green so dark is was almost hard to see. The forest seemed quiet; too quiet.

Quiet snickers could be heard from above. The Centrions looked up to find the branches lined with small creatures with big eyes, big ears and small noses. A wide grin crossed their faces making them appear evil.

"Gnomes," Daragorn snorted. "Prepare yourselves men, these little bastards are tricky."

"We heard you coming," a voice cackled out from the leaves above. The Centrions all looked around to find the source of the laughter. Daragorn and Luga were just as confused as their soldiers but kept a better head.

"Which one of you dares talk down to the Centrion race?" Luga's voice boomed in the quiet forest.

"You'll never know which one of us speaks." The sound came from the left. "You'll never know which one of us speaks." It was like an echo but it wasn't as this time the voice came from the right.

"Different voices," stated Luga. "One high, one low."

"However," Daragorn added, "we still have no idea to whom each voice belongs."

All the gnomes stood perfectly still on the branches, their faces all the same.

"Prepare for an attack. Once they…" It was too late to complete the sentence as the gnomes dropped down from above and swung from vines from all side. The Centrions were almost six times the size of the gnomes but this time the numbers were on the gnomes' side. Hundreds of gnomes attacked from the darkness above. Deep cuts began to appear in the legs and calves of the Centrions from the gnomes who surfaced from below. The Centrions swung blindly with their clubs and stabbed blind at the ground with their spears. The gnomes bit deep into the flesh of the Centrions and began ripping patches of their skin out.

"Stand your ground!" Daragorn ordered. "Swing your clubs over your heads and stomp the grounds at the same time."

"Do exactly as he orders," screamed Luga. The Centrions did as instructed and began to hear bones crack and crunch as they began to fight back evenly against the gnomes. It was too little too late. As the numbers seemingly began to fade more gnomes appeared in the trees above. The cycle seemed to continue and it was never-ending.

"Just how many of these little bastards are there!" Luga screamed.

More and more waves of gnomes appeared above while tinier screams of attack came from below. The waves grew larger and larger. Centrions began to fall heavily. Daragorn and Luga looked at the scattered bodies of Centrions lying strewn across the forest floor.

"Retreat!" both Daragorn and Luga screamed. The Centrions continued to fight just in order to retreat. They headed back toward the forest entrance with gnomes still attached to their backs. As sunlight started to flow back in through the cracks in the leaves above the dwarves let go. The battered, bruised and broken bodies of the remaining Centrions staggered out into the sunlight as they fell to the ground below. Some had to drag themselves back to the protection of the outlining boulders.

Daragorn and Luga gasped for air and Luga bellowed: "Back to Westershire and back to the Muddy Hills! We must regain our mentality and heal our bodies. We must reform and come back. There are too few of us. To fight Wickamore we need another platoon. We must tell Drayt and Gilf about the situation at hand."

"Luga, for now we rest," Daragorn said, "or we'll never make it back. Scrounge for food and boil the water from the sea to purify it. Without energy we will not survive." The Centrions looked at their slashed bodies. They tore off part of their garments and wrapped them tightly around their wounds to stop the life force from flowing out of their veins.

Luga and Daragorn looked at the tens of men left in their platoons. "We came in with hundreds, and left with fewer than sixty." As these words escaped the mouths of the generals, Luga hung his head low in shame.

"Yes, that is true," agreed Daragorn. "We were unprepared for the extreme nature of the gnome and underestimated the sheer vastness of their numbers. We stood no chance. The best thing we have going for us is that we escaped with some lives remaining, and we destroyed many of them. Krum will be very displeased. However, with this acquired knowledge, our next attack will be victorious.

Chapter 19

THE GIRL WHO MADE HER REMEMBER

Time passes and memories fade
Pillars break on foundation laid
But never forget those deep in your heart
They're there for always once from the start
They spark a light that time had darkened
And fuel the memory that now had harkened

Krum's massive hand gripped tightly around Mallory's arm as she was thrown onto an open wooden wagon and tied down with ropes as thick as chains. Lee and Koel were wound together, back-to-back and laid down in a separate wagon. The soldiers accompanying Krum controlled the wagons as he sat in the back with Mallory Bones. Her widened eyes screamed as her gagged mouth was stuffed with a cloth that had a nasty taste and an even nastier stench. Krum stared deep into her eyes.

"Who are you?" he said with an even tone, looking at her blonde hair and then back to her eyes again. "You're not from this world, that's evident enough, but who are you and where did you come from?" He was talking more to himself than Mallory. He looked into her eyes again. "If I take the cloth out, do you promise to answer my questions and promise not to scream, because if you scream I'm going to kill you where you stand?" Her eyes closed in confusion. "Whatever, you get my point." She thought for a minute and nodded. "Good," he said and pulled the dirty, foul cloth from her mouth. She breathed in a deep breath of cleaner air. "Now, who are you? We'll start with that."

"My name is Melanie. Melanie Rose." Mallory coughed and gathered more air in. "I come from another world called Earth." She coughed again and gasped trying to refill her lungs fully.

"Yes," said Krum, "I've heard of this other world." He looked into her eyes with a stony expression. His gaze demanded her attention.

"How? How have you?..." she asked.

"You're not the first visitor to Everworld, Melanie, and there's a good chance you won't be the last." He looked around surveying the landscape to catch his bearings. "Now," he continued, "why have you come to this world?"

"I didn't mean to. I bought a random book and showed up here after opening the cover." She kept hidden the fact she had unknow-ingly used the pendant as a means of traveling. She assumed he'd find the pendant at some point in time soon anyways.

"That doesn't just happen, Melanie. There needs to be some sort of object or artifact that allows travel between worlds, which leads me to my third question." Mallory's heart began to race, she knew what was coming. "What is tied around your neck?" Her heart sank.

"Bring it out or I will cut it off. Do you really want a knife to your neck?"

Mallory's shaking hand reached into her shirt top where she pulled out the circular emblem which included the letters MT. She had switched the vial to her pocket and the emblem to the necklace for safekeeping just before their capture. "This emblem was attached to the book. I realized it could be taken off. I held it in one hand and opened the book with the other. I swear I had no idea…"

"Yes, that I believe. Give it here," he demanded. Mallory handed the pendant over to the leader of the Centrion. Her hand, shaking, returned to her side.

How will I ever get home? she thought to herself. I hope Lee and Koel wake soon from their slumber. They had been knocked unconscious. She thought she saw Lee stir for a second but her imagination had taken control. He lay still, dead as a log, but breathing nonetheless.

"That's enough questions for now. Once we get back to the castle there will be time for more. I'm sure the queen would love to see the traveler she demanded us to kidnap in person."

"Queen?" she questioned aloud. "Which queen? How did she know about me being here?"

"Her majesty is a sorceress. She can find anyone, anywhere, at any time she desires. Now, enough talk before I decide whether or not to stuff this rag back into your mouth." He sat back and stared at her, contemplating Mallory. "Your name is not really Melanie," he said. Her heart skipped a beat and her lower lip trembled slightly but enough for Krum to see it happen. "We will find out soon enough. In all honesty I would have done the same thing. We'll arrive at the castle before nightfall.

Mallory took one last look around at the surroundings as she and her fellow guardians rode silently to the Castle of Shadows.

Upon arrival at the castle, Krum and his soldiers woke the unconscious elf and Natarian by tossing water onto them. They awoke with small headaches from the clubs that had blacked them out.

Lee and Koel looked around. "M…" Lee started to say.

"No!" Mallory screamed. She shook her head. Lee caught on and bit his lip hard enough to make it bleed.

With their hands tied behind their backs, the three captives made their way to the castle doors. In the evening the Castle of Shadows looked like a silhouette against the little sky there was that peaked through the dense clouds that hung above. Made of a black stone known only to Everworld, the castle seemed to rise forever. Pillars and turrets stood firmly in the corners of the walkway walls that connected the castle border. A large door made its presence known as the grand entrance to such a remarkable building. Krum and his men carried the captives to the big ironclad doors. The guards saluted the leader and stood at attention until Krum spoke.

"At ease," he said. "We have captured the young girl at the orders of the Queen of Darkness. Open the gates and let us pass to deliver the prisoners." The guards opened the door and stepped aside as Krum led the way into the Castle of Shadows.

It was dark and damp. The castle had its own peculiar odor. The odor was neither pleasant nor unpleasant. Mallory and Koel had trouble seeing anything but Lee's sharp eyes had enough strength to gather some of the surroundings. The beady eyes of the Centrions were used to the dark and could find their way no problem.

Passageway after passageway, turn after turn, staircase after staircase Mallory, Koel, and Lee found themselves being brought farther and farther into the castle. Just when Mallory thought she would be swallowed in darkness forever a small light began to glow a short distance away: firelight. Two torches could be seen on either side of a beautifully carved door where two more guards stood watch, swords in hand and heavily armored.

"Cainus and Rem; we have brought the captives as her majesty ordered. Please notify the queen of their arrival to the castle and that they stand captive on the other side of the door." The two soldiers did as instructed. They entered the room where they found the queen standing on her balcony looking out into the horizon.

"Excuse me, your majesty. Krum has captured and delivered the young girl and two others alongside her. We assume they were her guardians. One is an elf, the other a Natarian."

Morgana turned around with a smile on her face. The Dark Queen beamed with delight. "Finally. Bring them in." A greedy smile never left her face. The two soldiers returned to their post and instructed Krum to bring them in. Lee was pushed in first, Koel followed. Mallory entered last and Morgana's eyes expanded to the point of popping out of her skull. "I…impossible," she whispered. Her heart began racing and her entire body shook with devastating understanding. She walked slowly over to Mallory, completely ignoring Lee and Koel. Mallory stared back at Morgana, looking her over from head to foot until something inside her shot her like lightning. Where did she know this face from? Just the mere presence of the queen sent electrical shocks through her body.

"Hair color like straw and eyes that blow away the clouds that dim the sky." Morgana's words came out soft and sweet. Krum had never heard the queen talk with such softness. His gaze switched from Morgana to Mallory over and over. Her hands trembled as she reached for Mallory's hair. She felt the silky blonde hair flow off her fingers. She caressed the smooth skin of Mallory's cheek line down to her chin. Mallory flinched. A jolt shot through her body as she backed away quickly. "Girl," her voice became stiffer and controlled more authority. "Tell me your name, now! You share the same face as someone dear to me; someone from my past. I will know if you are lying so do not test me. I have more power than you could ever imagine."

With waves of adrenaline and tingles passing through Mallory's body she opened her mouth to speak but nothing came out.

"I said speak! Now!" Morgana's voice boomed and echoed against the dark stone walls.

Mallory flinched again. Koel and Lee looked over at Mallory and knew there was nothing they could do. "My name," she said, "is Mallory Bones."

Chapter 20

VISIONS OF WAR

Sometimes you just know.
Sometimes you just believe.
And in the hands of trust you throw
What you trust you can achieve.

All was quiet in Algernon except for the fountain that lay in the center of Algernon. The morning was dim, which if you asked the natives was a sure sign of trouble, as low clouds hung over the stone and grassy land. The Elven Queen Evana looked out of her window down onto the fog covered grounds, her left hand clasped to her chest. She felt a wickedness approaching, and in her mind she heard sounds of roaring and shrieking, metal clanging and drums banging. War. That's what it was and she knew it. This darkness, though, was far greater than that. She felt a destruction and devastation that she had never dreamed of. Her brow trembled and her breath quickened before she was able to snap out of the nightmare she was stuck in. She turned from the window and fled down the staircase inside her home to a young male warrior who stood guard just inside her door.

"Feyler," Evana gasped as she reached the bottom of the staircase." Feyler rushed to her side as Evana collapsed to the floor.

"My queen!" Feyler responded as he helped her up easily.

"Feyler, we must act now!" Her voice was full of panic. "Danger is approaching and destruction will be upon us if we do not call for help."

"What is wrong? Is Lee in trouble?" Feyler asked.

"I know not of Lee Odion or of Mallory Bones current whereabouts but something is coming to threaten this village and bring devastation to our people. I fear for all of Everworld," the queen said as she stared into Feyler's eyes.

"What will you have me do, your majesty?" Feyler continued to hold her upright. She brushed him off lightly indicating she was alright to hold her own balance.

"Send Ezer and another of our warriors out to the Valley of Shadows. Call upon the tribal king and do so with honor and respect. Have Ezer tell him of my feelings and of my vision and what I believe to be coming. I fear his people are in danger as well. Fighting together may be the only chance we have left. When Michael Bones helped end the war we swore an oath to never go back to war unless a common danger threatened Everworld and in such an instance to fight side-by-side. I know there must be questions but I ask you do this without question and I will answer those questions you may have in time."

Without another moment's hesitation the loyal elf left the queen's side to report to Ezer the instructions the queen had given him.

Ezer was walking around the grounds of Algernon and was near the fountain when Feyler happened upon him.

"Ezer!" Feyler's sense of urgency could be heard in his voice.

"Yes, Feyler, what is it? You seem to be troubled," Ezer said.

"Indeed," Feyler responded and grasped both Ezer's shoulders with his hands. "The queen sent me to find you at once and has a message she desperately needs you to give to the king of the tribal lands."

"High Chief Annikan?" Ezer's voice was full of questioned tone. "What does Queen Evana need of him?"

"She spoke of ill feelings and troubled thoughts. She believes war is closing in upon us once again." Feyler then turned his head and looked upon the fountain with the initials M.B. carved into the stone pillar in the middle. Ezer looked over at the initials as well. Both looked back into each other's eyes. "Out of respect for Everworld's savior we promised to only fight in war alongside our brothers of the Valley of Shadows. Bring no weapons as to pose no threat and with the most respect you can muster ask permission to speak to the high chief. Say that you come in the name of Queen Evana. She asked me to pose no questions and to hurry. Please take another warrior with you, again, devoid of weapons, and proceed to the valley at once." He released Ezer's shoulders. Ezer nodded and rushed off quickly to do the duty Queen Evana had assigned to him. Once Ezer had recruited Lanzer to join him on the errand the two elves set off immediately to the Valley of Shadows.

Feyler returned to the queen's home where she stood in the doorway with both hands clasped to her chest.

"Ezer has been sent. It's safe to assume he's gone to find Lanzer; those two work the best together in times of need."

"I wish them both the best," the queen said. "I fear the entire fate of Everworld will depend on Chief Annikan trusting in my beliefs. We have fought alongside them in the past and the hope is that they will come in arms to fight alongside us again." Feyler turned around to face in the same direction as the queen.

Ezer and Lanzer quickly reached the Valley of Shadows. Ahawi's soldiers, seeing them come from a distance, encircled them as they did Mallory and Lee and every other passerby. The lands were truly highly protected.

Ahawi spoke: "Speak of your reason to come to our valley, elves of Algernon."

Ezer spoke: "We come in peace but tell of war. We come unarmed. We come in the name of Queen Evana and ask humbly to speak to High Chief Annikan. Our queen speaks of ill feelings and of nightmarish visions. We plead you let us speak to your high chief."

Ahawi rode around the two elves mounted on cloppers and saw they were unarmed. "Anything you can tell the chief you can tell me." Ahawi stared at Ezer.

Lanzer spoke up: "'Tis true that we can, however, our queen asks that we speak directly to the chief. Put us in shackles if you must and be present yourself at the time of our telling but please allow us this special privilege. I beg you in the name of the entire elven race. He unmounted his clopper and motioned for Ezer to do the same. He dropped to one knee and crossed his arm over his chest and lowered his head. He then stood up and placed both arms out in front of him together, wrists up. "My wrists await the shackles, but my lungs and tongue await the chief."

Ahawi nodded and spoke: "Please remount your cloppers and follow us into the village. I will tell Chief Annikan you ask for his presence in the name of your queen and of your people. I will tell him you come unarmed and that I fear nothing of you two. Your intentions seem pure."

"Era yeht," responded Ezer as he climbed back atop his clopper and then looked into the eyes of the head warrior. Ahawi nodded and led the two elves into the village.

Ezer and Lanzer waited patiently accompanied by some of the warriors as Ahawi emerged from the tent followed by the king. Ezer and Lanzer sighed, relieved to find the chief accepted their company.

"Elves of Algernon, what brings you to the Valley of Shadows?" Annikan's voice was full of authority.

Lanzer spoke with a voice of stone as to assure his statements: "We come in the name of our queen, Evana. She speaks of ill feelings and visions of war. Last time our queen felt these she was right and all of Everworld was almost destroyed. She asks in the name of Michael Bones that you fight alongside us as he requested after his help in ending the last Great War. She doesn't know exactly who, where or when the enemy will strike, but she knows it's soon."

"If there is trouble and we do fight alongside each other who will protect our villages? Which village will be left open for an attack?"

"Fi yo yam," Ezer said. Speaking the old language caught the attention of the chief. "There are only three people in my village that can speak the language of old. "Dna yo," he said, "ma eno fo meht." Ezer unmounted and bowed as Lanzer had done prior.

Annikan nodded. "Your respect is appreciated. Rise up and speak."

Ezer rose up and looked up in the tall chief's eyes. "If one of our tribes vacated our lands and for the time being and resided in Caidel then there would be no one for an opposing army to attack or kill. The lands of your valleys make a far better battleground then the grassy-stone hills of Algernon. Men, women and child of both lands could be sent to Caidel and we could fight the army or armies together in the wide lands here. I imagine that war on your lands is the last thing you want, but for battle strategy purposes it's the far better option." He looked over at Ahawi who nodded in agreement.

"The elf is right, Annikan."

Annikan stood silently mulling over all the information the elf had unloaded on him like a bombshell. "I've never had a reason to doubt Queen Evana before and there is no need to start now. Who is it that she believes will attack us?"

"Of that I do not know and I have high doubt she does either for then I would surely know. We can only act on a feeling of a queen who last time was accurate and helped save our entire world from a perilous fate," Ezer stated.

Annikan thought again. "Be off then," Annikan said. Ezer's heart rose. "Go and tell Queen Evana of our plan. Tell her to vacate the elven people to Caidel and I will instruct the same of mine. Does she know how long until the attack?"

"No, but she believes it to be soon. I believe if she sent me off right away it couldn't be more than a day or two away."

"Go, then, and hurry!" Annikan said and bowed to them. Ezer remounted his clopper and both elves took off back to Algernon.

Upon arrival back to the village, Ezer and Lanzer told the queen of their discussion with High Chief Annikan. Queen Evana and Feyler listened and nodded in agreeance to the best plan of action.

"Gather all to the fountain and I will tell our people of the predicament." Feyler, Ezer and Lanzer dispersed quickly and began to collect everyone to the fountain. Evana made her way back up the stairs to the window where the visions first happened. She would speak from that window and tell her people of troubled times ahead.

After time had passed a crowd had gathered near the fountain in anticipation of the news their queen had for them. Evana appeared at the window of the upper story of her home and looked down upon the innocent elven people and spoke. Back in the Valley of Shadows Chief Annikan did the same. Both the elven people and the Natarians set out that night for refuge in the central kingdom of Caidel. The elven warriors not leading their people to safety mounted their cloppers and followed their queen and their warriors back to the Valley of Shadows where another fight would ensue. Another great war had indeed broken out in Everworld, and this time Michael Bones would not be there. He lay sick on Earth slowly withering away, barely able to move at this point, barely able to speak.

The elves reached the Valley of Shadows where the Chief Annikan greeted Queen Evana. Battle plans and hopes came to life as they waited for their enemies to close in upon them.

Chapter 21

KINGDOMS FALL, A QUEEN'S FATE

Even the most skilled can be beaten.
Even the mightiest of kingdoms fall.
Even those who fight together can do nothing at all.
When your best men have been sent away
When your kingdom awaits in fate's hands
It can be defended, it can be rebuilt, and
the two sides replenish their lands.

Two kingdoms now side to fight a foe.
A common goal for a reclaimed peace to grow.
Together they die, together they live, in a hope to stop the fire
That spreads across an old world's empire.

Queen and Chief stand hand in hand in combat with the rest.
They fight on, in hopes of life till life's essence leaves their breast.

The crooked few who start this fight will see it to its end.
Even if it means defeat, it's better that they're dead.

Overcast skies draped in clouds of melancholy loomed overhead; a precursor to the end of a battle that would soon ensue. A large army stood along the edges of the Valley of Shadows. Dragu and Stoval stood side-by-side. The mass of their combined armies stood behind them. Together they would destroy the plain's warriors and together they would push on into the Black Forrest Hills. They believed in their hearts that it was finally time for the Centrions to reign. Their time was now and nothing would hold them back. They believed everything was going perfectly, until the fight began.

Deep vibrations rattled the air as the blasting sounds of war horns boomed like thunder across the flat plains. Dragu raised his right arm in the air and dropped it pointing forward with the confidence of a god. The ground trembled like an earthquake as the heavily armored armies marched toward the Natarians and elves. The elves would be a special surprise as Dragu and Stoval were not expecting the Natarians to have an accompanying army. On the other hand, Gorga and Kaen would come to be gifted with their own surprise.

"Forward men!" exclaimed Stoval. "For the Centrion race!"

The clouds that hung over the Valley of Shadows stretched all the way to the southwestern portions of Everworld. This slash of clouds acted as a scar, one that marred the beauty of Everworld. But it showed truth – Everworld was in the midst of war, a war that Mallory Bones would soon be a part of – a war far different from that her father helped end.

Unlike their counterparts marching in the Valley of Shadows, these two soldiers surrounded the village of Algernon in the hope of an all-out attack that would be as swift as possible. Gorga turned to face his army. As he opened his mouth to speak from the corner of his eye he spotted a Centrion come blazing, running fast. He turned to the oncoming Centrion who collapses to one knee.

"Lord Gorga, I come bearing news. Algernon is deserted. There are none there!"

Gorga's eyes widen. "How do you know this?"

"Both the elves and the Natarians have gathered together to fight side-by-side in the Valley of Shadows. Somehow they knew we were coming."

Gorga turned facing across the deserted Algernon. "Kaen!" he screamed. His voice echoed throughout the landscape. "We have been tricked! Algernon is empty. The elves have travelled to the valley to fight alongside the Natarians. We must move out now or else Dragu and Stoval will surely fail and our chance to rule over this godforsaken world will fall. Our attempts will be in vain."

Overlooking Algernon from a mountain of rock wall Kaen's eyes narrowed. He turned to his army and uttered a single world. A deep voice full of hate and as cold as icebound stone growled out, "Move!"

Queen Evana and Chief Annikan stood in front of their soldiers. Ahawi and Feyler stood behind them in front of their respective tribes. Behind them, massed together, was a brand new element of destruction – the two strongest armies in all of Everworld standing together in arms, waiting for a fight – the fight – that would decide the fate of their beloved world. Ahawi turned around to face a sea of mixed people.

"Brothers. Sisters. Today we stand together in hopes to defend our world, Everworld. Let the thunder you feel from the ground beneath your feet serve as a reminder of the strength of the foe that comes to take away our way of life, if not our lives entirely. But remember that we are stronger. Our hearts and our desire to survive and give a peaceful life to those we love is stronger than the strength of the evil that lies within the hearts of the Centrions. They crave power. These creatures carry the heavy burden of the seven deadly sins that lie within their hearts. They forget their freedoms, all in vain – a vanity designated by the rule over all others. They believe death is nobler than the life they lead now. Look upon your fellow man and remember why you fight. Let their blood flow through your veins and allow yours to act as a life force to theirs. Today we fight for all that we love. Today we fight for Everworld!" She raised her bow to a scream of cheers that rose from the masses that listened to her speak. Feyler unsheathed his bow and did the same. Ezer drew his sword and held it up high.

Feyler spoke as the cheer died down: "Today we are short two brothers, and for them we fight as well. We will have them back, safe and in one piece. We shall bring back Mallory Bones safe and in one piece. And after today we will bring back the shattered remains of Everworld to one piece. Allow Lee Odion and Koel Lo'Hota to fight with you inside your hearts. Allow their leadership to empower you, to will you to fight on. For this will not be an easy fight. You will grow tired, weary and hungry. But you will succeed. We will succeed. Now draw your weapons and prepare for battle!" The last of these words were yelled with force.

Queen Evana spoke, "From the hearts and minds of all the elves of Algernon, we thank you all."

Chief Annikan Tawah spoke: "From the hearts and minds of the Natarian warriors of the valleys, we thank you all. On the drop of the queen's hand the fight begins. Meet our enemy head on for that is the way of the warrior." Evana and Annikan looked at each other and nodded their heads then turned to face the dark mass that steamrolled ever closer. Evana raised her hand in the air. A loud cry of war raged from the Centrions. The queen's hand dropped to point towards the evil that set upon the elves and Natarians. The prey became the predator as bodies raced past the queen and high chief with the generals leading the way. Their own screams, too loud to be silenced by the clouds above, echoed through the plains. A brand new war had begun.

Soundwaves smashed together in the air as bodies collided with thuds below. The clinking and clanking of words, shields and armor accompanied screeches and cries of war. A sharp cry splintered the air as Dragu's blade came slashing at a downward angle and sliced open the stomach of an elven warrior. Thick blue blood trickled out like syrup. As the warrior fell to the ground Dragu stepped onto his body, crushing his chest, the bones snapping underneath like a brittle fall leaf.

At the sound of the scream Ezer let out a cry of utter rage. The sound of the elven warrior's despair filled the air, drowning out all other sound for a brief moment as he slashed his own blade through the open neck slot of a Centrion's armor that he stood battling. A deep emerald green blood cascaded like a flood down the cold steel that covered the Centrion's body. The Centrion fell to the cold ground gasping for breath. A fire raged in Ezer's eyes as he stood above the dying soldier, his sword drawn. He grasped the handle tight, the tip of the sword pointed down. He raised the hilt as high as possible with the absolute intention of dropping it hard and fast in the left eye of the pathetic creature that lay below. Just before the action took place an arrow whizzed by in his peripheral.

Another scream echoed out as the arrow shot by Ezer plunged deep into the throat of a Centrion. The booming cry of the Centrion was silenced as the arrow sliced through the back of the throat and stuck out like a jester with a fake arrow-through-the-head prop, except it was much more real and deadly. The heavy body of the Centrion fell to the ground at the same time a light weight was placed on the left shoulder of Ezer. Ezer stood frozen in fear as a voice calmly spoke from behind, "watch your back brother."

Ezer turn around slowly, sword grasped ready to swing. His rapidly beating heart began to slow. Feyler grabbed him by the wrist and pulled him forward just in time to avoid the axe swing of a Centrion. The natural battle skills of Ezer took over as he swiftly turned the sword in his hand and plunged it backwards into the beating heart of a Centrion that left himself wide open. Ezer's eyes never left Feyler's.

"Remember," Feyler spoke calmly as he stared deep into the eyes of a young warrior who'd never been in anything even close to war, "never let anger become your guide or your only victory will be defeat."

"Thank you, Feyler!" Ezer created a fist and raised it to his forehead before the two split off again and returned to the action of battle.

The large ears of Stoval picked up on all the sounds emanating from the battle raging around him. His intelligence kept him at bay staying toward the back of the pack as his platoon fought on in front of him. He never strayed from the fight but he knew his importance as a captain to the Centrions – and the reality that his death would be a big blow to the command ranks.

"Dragu may be smart, but the half-pint always allows the importance of his position to slip by him. He's a master commander during battle but his strategy drowns in his recklessness." The words were mumbled under Stoval's breath as a Natarian warrior's sword was split in half by the axe hammer that Stoval commanded. The broken sword was thrust to the ripped and torn ground of Everworld. The

Valley of Shadows was slowly becoming riddled with puddles of teal as a bloodbath took place right before his beady black eyes. Stoval contributed to the filling of this new sea as he picked up the Natarian by the skull and slit his throat. He tossed the warrior away like a ragdoll without looking back.

Mighty steeds coated in spots and stripes of green blood raged through the front lines of the Centrion Army. The whinny and neigh of the steeds seemed drowned compared to the screams of the men and women fighting on ground level. Ahawi's bow bounced along her back as she rode between creatures of both races. Her hair trailed in the wind and came to a stop as she came upon a small opening amongst the masses and was met by Dragu.

"State your name!" Ahawi growled. Her dark red hair flowing down her back leaving her furred brow and clenched teeth fully visible.

"My name matters not to you. It will only matter to the future Centrion race when I knock you off your pet and crush you into the ground," Dragu laughed. "And after I kill you I'll kill your horse and eat it for dinner once we've won."

"You have absolutely no idea who I am. Allow me to introduce myself." She raised her bow and loaded it with an arrow so straight it could match a ruler. The feathers on the end were made from that of a white faracaw. Those feathers would soon be dyed green as she pulled the strings back and tightened the string of the bow set to kill.

Dragu laughed again and his cocky voice spat from his toothy grin. "You think that itsy bitsy arrow is going to harm me? It won't even pierce my…" But his words were cut short as he stood frozen in time. There were two quick whiffs in the air and everything went black for the Centrion. From each eye jutted a separate arrow. Dragu stumbled and fell onto his back, sprawled out on the dirt below.

"My name is Ahawi. I am the head warrior of the Natarian people and we fight with honor and with pride. We will win." She remounted her war horse and set off to fight alongside those she promised to defend.

The fighting raged on. Swordsmen fought valiantly as arrows flew over heads and shoulders. They flew into limbs, both connected and severed. Stoval, unaware of Dragu's death, crept around the perimeter of the battle staying just inside the fight as to not draw too much attention. Finally, he came upon the fresh corpse of Dragu. He plucked the arrows from his eyes. He mumbled one word, "pathetic," and continued on his way to where Annikan and Evana stood. As he rounded the final edge he peered out and saw his opening and took it. He launched himself out of the crowd of bodies. He ran toward the two leaders full blast. The small group of Natarians and elves surrounding their leaders ran like a moving wall toward the Centrion. They were no match for the large boar as he clubbed them aside dealing deadly blows to the sides of their heads. After the group had been eliminated he continued on his determined path to defeat the chief of the Natarians and the queen of the 'damned elves'.

A quick jolt of pain shot out of the right arm of Stoval. Stuck in the thick boar skin was an arrow. Feyler's footsteps fell like lightning as he streaked across the battlefield towards the beast. Stoval snapped the arrow in half, leaving half the arrow inside his arm. He turned to face the racing elf. He drew his club high into the air and pretended to swing down. Feyler made an attempt to dodge by sliding under Stoval's arm, but instead of swinging down Stoval jolted his right knee upwards. All of the air in Feyler's lungs came exploding out. He gasped for air as his hands unclenched and he dropped his bow. He fell to the ground on his hands and knees. He tried again to gasp for air and was kicked ruthlessly in the ribs, tumbling him over. Stoval reached down and picked him up by his neck. He ripped off the dagger attached to his hip and looked Feyler dead in his eyes.

Feyler was tossed back to the ground. "Your queen will perish beneath my might! I only wish you could watch." These were the last words that Feyler heard. Stoval swung up his mighty axe hammer and slammed it hard into Feyler's skull. He left his hammer where it lay atop the skull of the dead Elvan warrior. He picked up and unsheathed the dagger he ripped off Feyler's belt and held it up with a grin that split from large ear to large ear. He continued to advance towards the queen and chief. Annikan stepped in front of Evana. Stoval stopped a foot away and laughed in the face of the chief. "You have absolutely no idea what I'm capable of, Annikan." His last name he spoke with spite. He sneered and jumped. He propelled himself over the head of Annikan and Evana and landed behind her. Frozen by such an acrobatic feat, Annikan's legs turned to lead and the biological wires of Evana seemed to short out. Stoval landed on one knee and rose up, dagger in hand. Without a moment's hesitation he stepped up to Evana and raised her by her throat with his left hand. "There's only one queen, Evana, and that's Morgana." Stoval bellowed a grotesque laugh and continued, "all hail, Queen Morgana!" The dagger in his right hand thrust forward and into the stomach of Evana. Evana looked down, unable to speak or breathe. Blood began to trickle from the corners of her mouth and lips and eventually began to pour as her head began to droop. She looked down at her wound and back up into Stoval eyes as hers turned to glass. He twisted the dagger and pulled it out letting her drop to a bloody, blue mess.

Annikan screamed so loud it rumbled over the landscape, smothering all other sounds of war. "Queen Evana!" He clenched his left fist and from his back drew a bow with his right.

Ezer turned to see the queen dead upon the ground and cried out. He ran towards Stoval only to be held back by Ahawi.

"Let me go! I must be by her side. I must…"

"Ezer, she is dead. You'll only kill yourself if you try to fight him alone. Chief Annikan can take him out alone as long as we keep the others at bay." She released his shoulder.

"My queen," he cried the words as tears tumbled from his eyes. His shoulders rocked as he wept. After a moment he wiped his tears and his eyes turned to fire. The fire within his eyes would spark a new one within his heart. He looked up into the solemn eyes of Ahawi. "Let's end this." He said through gritted teeth.

Ahawi looked down towards him and nodded.

Annikan nocked an arrow into his bow.

"You do realize that your precious bow's arrow cannot pierce my skin or armor. You have nothing. There is no way for you to defend yourself. You are outmatched," Stoval sneered as he dropped the dagger and picked up the bloody axe hammer off Feyler's crushed skull. "But, if you insist," Stoval said with a smile, "I will kill you as well."

The wind began to pick up as if the air captured the tension. They circled each other measuring each other's size. Attempts to predict movements shot through their minds, calculating at incredible speeds. Two masters of battle seemingly frozen in time. The patience of Annikan paid off as Stoval was the first to make a move. He rushed head on and swung his axe hammer hard from the left. Annikan dodged it quickly by ducking underneath and slid to the right, popping back up into the same defensive stance he began in, arrow still knocked and string pulled tight. Annikan waited again until Stoval sneered and swung a second time. Again Annikan dodged, this time sliding to the left before firing the first arrow. Being at close distance gave Stoval no time to move, but his thick hide propelled the arrow backwards bouncing it off like a rubber ball. It fell to the ground and stuck in the mud below.

Stoval grinned wide. "You're wasting your time, chief," he chuckled. "There's no way the arrow can penetrate…"

Before Stoval had a chance to finish Annikan rushed him and slid his boot down the side of Stoval's leg shaving off some of the tough skin, softening the spot. He jumped back as he simultaneously knocked another arrow into the bow and fired rapidly at the outer knee on the newly exposed soft spot. The arrow stuck in. Stoval closed his eyes for only a split second gritting his teeth in pain, but a split second was all Annikan needed as he jumped toward Stoval again and smashed the bottom of his shoe into the end of the arrow. With a squish and a rip the arrow tore through the knee, the ends of the arrow protruding on each side. Stoval's left knee buckled under him as he let out a mighty roar.

While down on his torn knee he pulled the arrow out and growled again. He stood back up, his toughness on parade. He lifted the axe hammer and began to wing it slowly over his head like a tornado. Faster and faster the axe hammer swung until it seemed as if he could be propelled with it, like Thor flying through the air by throwing his mighty hammer, Mjölnir. He released the axe hammer and let it fly. It was just slightly off the mark as it passed just over Annikan's right shoulder cutting off a large portion of his long, red hair. Any lower and Annikan's right arm would have been yards away in a puddle of green Centrion blood. Stoval grunted in disgust with himself.

Annikan walked up to Stoval. He stopped just out of arm's reach and stared deep into his eyes. Stoval lunged for him and missed propping himself back onto one knee. He pulled the largest arrow he had out of the quiver that hung on his back. He knocked the arrow and pulled back tight on the bow string. He opened his mouth to speak. "Dna won," he spoke in the voice of old, "won tu eid." He released the tension as the arrow flew forward in a flash. It entered the Centrion's skull through the center of the nose, splitting his skull like a banana peel. Stoval fell to the ground, green thick blood trickling from the cracks.

"Ahawi!" cried Annikan. She turned to him at the sound of her name. "Finish this." Ahawi nodded and let out a cry of war. The real war would wage on for hours and the great Centrion race would continue to crumble and fall.

Chapter 22

HIDING IN CAIDEL

Wicked with lies, the past stings
Carried to tower on golden wings
When truth is at hand, actions show
How to deal with issues from long ago.
Stories unfold in aging time
Like sand turns to stone; an ancient crime.

Her heart beat hard inside her chest. The silence allowed her pulse to pound like echoes of her past drumming back from long lost memory. A single tear began to form in her left eye before she blinked it away.

"Mallory? Mallory Bones?" The words came out choked.

Mallory hesitated and replied, "Yes?"

Morgana walked quickly to where Mallory stood and placed both hands on Mallory's shoulders. She bent down and her eyes searched deep into the crystal blue of Mallory's eyes. Another tear woke from the corner of her eyes and strolled down her cheek. In slow motion it seemed to fall right onto Mallory's cheek. Before Mallory could wipe the tear away Morgana pulled her into her embrace. She stood eyes closed holding her child to her chest. Awkward silence blasted throughout the room.

Mallory stood with her arms pinned to her side not knowing how to react. "Excuse me, Queen Morgana, but why are you hugging me?"

"Mallory, oh Mallory, my little girl," she said.

Mallory's eyes first expanded then her brow furrowed. Her fists clenched together as she spoke. "I don't know how you're aware of my mother dying, but how dare you mock her. You're despicable."

"You don't understand, Mallory. It's me. It's me, your mother."

Mallory stood in silence unsure of how to respond. After a minute she spoke, "No you're not. My mother's dead!" Her voice rose and fell with each word, her tone full of anger. She pushed away from the queen's embrace. "She left me and my dying father because she couldn't handle the stress. She let her past get the best of her and she couldn't handle the responsibility."

Morgana's shoulders slumped and she cupped her hands over her face and wept silently.

"Why do you play this game? My mother is dead."

"I'm not dead," came Morgana's response. "You can see in front of you that I'm standing right here."

"You do share her name, that is true, and your look is similar except for your hair and your eyes. My Mother possesses hair like mine and her eyes are not yellow. Humans from Earth do not have yellow eyes."

"I can explain all that in time if you give me a chance." The Dark Queen was pleading with a young girl. All in the room remained silent until Krum spoke up.

"Your majesty," he said cautiously, "is what you say true? Is this young visitor from Earth your child?"

"I swear it in the name of Evelyn that Mallory Bones is my little girl."

"Prove it!" demanded Mallory. "What is my middle name?"

"Ellen." The reply was quick and without question.

"You're a sorceress. That's easy enough for you to figure out." Mallory thought for a second. "What did you give me for my fifth birthday?"

"A doll I found at Aunt Miriam's Porcelain Treasures. She looked just like you." Morgana's hands were folded together and held to her chest. "Do you believe me now?"

"Answer one more question to prove it. This is a question that you can't use any magical power to answer. If you truly are my mother, why did you run away leaving me and leaving my father to die alone?"

Morgana's eyes dropped to the floor. She opened her mouth to speak but nothing but air came out.

"Exactly, you're not my mother." Mallory turned away and walked over to Lee. "Lee," she said looking at him then turned to Koel. "Koel," she said softly, "let's get out of here."

"Where do you think you're going?" Krum moved in front of the doorway blocking it with his enormous size.

"Krum," Morgana said with softness and sadness he'd never heard, "allow them to leave."

"But, your majesty?"

"I said let them leave." There was no anger in this tone. There was only frustration, disappointment and sadness.

"The girl can leave but the other two stay," Krum said, interjecting his own belief and wishes.

"Do not force me to call for Crimson," her voice raising on the word "not".

Krum sneered, his lip curled and he stepped aside. The three travelers exited the queen's room and began to walk downstairs.

An older man in gray robes was walking up the staircase when he almost bumped into the trio.

"Oh, excuse me," a voice spoke. Mallory looked up. The eyes of Crimson seemed to glow in the darkness of the castle.

"We were just leaving," Mallory said.

"The Dark Queen has allowed it," Lee added.

"Of course," Crimson said with an extension of the arm. "My name is Crimson. I'm a wizard here and I serve her majesty."

"My name is Mallory Bones."

"Who are your friends?" Crimson asked.

"Not that it matters to you," Lee cut in. "My name is Lee Odion."

"And you are?" Crimson looked over at Koel who stood staring at him.

"My name is Koel Lo'Hota."

"Pleasure to meet you all," Crimson said and grinned. "I'm sure we'll meet again," he said in an airy voice.

"What's that supposed to mean?" Mallory barked.

"Nothing, little mistress. I offer my most sincere apologies. I wish you travelers well." With a nod of his head he finished ascending the staircase and turned towards Morgana's room. The other three continued their way down the stars and followed the path out of the castle, carefully retracing the steps they remembered from when they were brought here as prisoners.

They came upon the main doors to the castle and opened it to their expected freedom. Instead of being questioned on why they were leaving by the two guards that were there prior, they found them lying face down on the dirt of Everworld.

"What happened here?" Lee questioned, bending down to examine the guards for a reason behind their unfortunate situation. From behind, Lee heard two quick grunts and turned to see Mallory and Koel knocked unconscious, before he too was struck from behind. He fell unconscious to the ground, joining the two guards, Mallory and Koel.

Two burly beings, completely human looking like they came straight from Earth, lifted Koel and Lee from the dirt and placed them inside a carriage pulled by two cloppers. A third man, bigger than the other two, bent down to pick up Mallory. He gently lifted her from the ground and laid her down inside the carriage on a bench of velvet. The three men exited and the man who picked up Mallory grabbed control of the reigns and set the cloppers in motion. They would travel to the capital of Everworld, Caidel, which was only a half-day's travel at most.

Several hours later Mallory woke up in a soft bed covered in white linen. Her eyes eased open as the light from the window aggravated her head. She still had a small headache from the bump she took that knocked her unconscious. In the corner of the room she saw three men gathered. Two of them were Koel and Lee, the other was a man of above-average size with dark, raven colored hair. She tried to push the covers down to exit the bed.

The big man was facing in her direction saw her stir and walked toward her. Koel and Lee followed. He kneeled at the side of her bed and spoke softly to her.

"Mallory, take it easy and don't move too fast. You probably still have a small headache."

"Where am I?" was all she could get out as she looked into his dark eyes.

"My name is Alder. I'm the prince of Caidel. Caidel is the center city of Everworld. Mallory looked over at Lee and Koel.

Koel came to her bedside and grabbed her hand. She took it and sat up readjusting herself against the headrest.

"How are you?" Lee asked.

"I'm okay, just a little sore. I'm confused. What happened and how did we end up here?"

"I take full responsibility for that," Alder spoke, his voice still pleasant and calm. "Two of my men and I knocked you three out to bring you back here. We needed you here and couldn't risk taking 'no' for an answer. I apologize and humbly ask for forgiveness. I can promise you that you are safe here and in good hands."

"He speaks the truth," Lee said. There is a lot to fill you in on. Once you are more awake and prepared to hear. Now you must eat."

"Ah, yes," Alder agreed. "I shall fetch you some food and drink." He left the room and appeared moments later with some bread and water.

During his brief absence Mallory spoke to Lee. "He is the prince of Everworld?"

"Yes," Lee said. "He is the prince of the Humanus. The Humanus are a race very similar to you humans on Earth," he reminded her.

"If he is the prince, where is the king?" She asked.

"The king passed away during the last great war. The very war your father helped stop."

"Why are we here Lee?"

Lee opened his mouth to respond but before he could get a word out Alder came back in with the bread and water.

"I know it's not much but I'm having the chefs prepare you a fresh meal now. Hopefully this can suffice until then. You're probably wondering what you're doing here, aren't you?"

Mallory nodded.

"As I told Lee and Koel while you slept, we have received word of another war that has broken out in Everworld. The Centrions seem to be the ones spearheading this war. We have reason to believe the war is already underway."

"What!" Mallory exclaimed, her eyes switching between Lee and Alder.

"All of the elven and Natarian civilians have gathered within our city walls. We have no news about the dwarves of Asenfall or the gnomes of Wickamore but we fear they may have already fallen. The Natarian and elven warriors have prepared for battle together in the Valley of Shadows. You three were brought here to keep you safe. Lee and Koel have asked to fight alongside their brothers and sisters but I insisted that they stayed. I fear that eventually the Centrions will reach Caidel. If Caidel falls all is lost and the Centrions will win this war." Alder paused for a brief second before he spoke again. "I'm sure you've heard of your father's deeds and doings?"

Mallory sat speechless. She shook her head unsure of what to say. She thought about her father. Her father! She slammed her hands to her pockets hoping to feel her vile full of the Water of Tears. She breathed a sigh of relief as her hands cupped around the tubular shape of the vile. She pulled it out and put it back on the necklace. She replied, "Yes, I have heard some of the things my father had done for Everworld. But I did not come to be in Everworld by his help or his hand. I came here by a book and an emblem on the book." The emblem! How could she forget? She closed her eyes and breathed out deep in frustration.

"Did this emblem detach from the book and share two letters?" Alder asked.

"Yes," Mallory answered, "but how did you know?"

"I know because in our sacred library we have the other book. There are two books and two emblems; one to travel here and one to travel back."

"But how did Morgana get here?"

"Queen Morgana of the Castle of Darkness?" Alder questioned.

"Yes," Mallory responded. "She claims to be my mother. My mother ran away two years ago and was never found. If it's true and she is her, how did she get here?"

"It's possible she used the emblem to get here. She trained under Evelyn, a sorceress, when she arrived. And with that knowledge travelled back to Earth, reattached the symbol and then used her powers to travel back here. You see, once you travel, the ability is engrained within you. You would no longer need the emblem."

"She really is my mother then," Mallory said as a fact, not a question. "Why would she come here?" Mallory blurted out.

"I do not know," Alder responded. "But what I do know is that we must protect Everworld from falling to the Centrions. After that we can search for and obtain answers to these other questions."

"So how do we go about that?" Mallory asked.

"Lee, Koel and I were in the process of discussing that when you woke up. I'll go get your food, it should be ready by now and after you have eaten and have energy again we can discuss our priorities and plans." Alder stood back up and exited the room for a second time.

"Mallory," Koel spoke, "I know you have many questions, but I give you a Natarian promise that the answers will come in time. Do you trust me?"

"Yes. Thank you Koel."

Koel nodded. He took Mallory's hand in his and squeezed it gently. Mallory smiled up at him and then over at Lee.

"Thank you both." They nodded back.

Alder re-entered the room with a silver platter with all sorts of food. He handed it to Mallory like breakfast in bed. It smelled heavenly to her. She thanked him and tried everything on the plate. Random thoughts of her dad popped into her head. Every minute wasted is another minute closer to his death. With this thought her heart sank and a frown split her face.

"You're worried about your father aren't you?" Alder asked. "Koel and Lee filled me in. What you're doing is very admirable and I promise as soon as we end this war I will do everything in my power to help you get back to your father as soon as possible."

"What do I do about my mother?" Mallory asked.

"That," Alder said, "is up to you."

Mallory looked down and grasped the vile on her chest again. Did she really want her mother back in her life after leaving her and her father like that? She had a lot to think about. "So, for now we hide in Caidel?" she asked.

"We strategize," Alder retorted. Mallory smiled.

"What is our course of action, Prince Alder?" Lee asked.

"We wait to see the steps the enemy takes first. We gather intelligence about the situation at large and how much destruction they've caused and we move on from there. I'll have some of my best men leave at once." Koel and Lee nodded to this.

A knock rapped on the door to the room. All four looked in the direction and there stood a tall man in all-white attire. He was old and grizzled but possessed an aura of immense power. Lee's eyes grew wide as he instantly fell to one knee. Koel, upon seeing Lee do this, fell to one knee as well.

"Azarim, it's good to see you again so soon." Alder bowed.

Back on Earth Michael Bones was busy entering the worst state of his life. He could barely breathe let alone move anymore. All of his focus and energy was spent on following Mallory's story.

"Morgana, he whispered. Somehow I just knew you were alive." A tear fell from his left eye.

Daniel entered the room to see tears rolling down his cheeks. "Michael!" he exclaimed.

"Don't worry, dad, I'm fine. Mallory is fine," he paused before finishing, "and even Morgana is fine." Daniel's brow furrowed in confusion.

"But Michael, she's dead." He was starting to question the mentality of his son. Any mental deterioration caused by the cancer was something he figured Michael would have to deal with eventually, and it would be a struggle to communicate.

Michael shook his head and reached the book out in a trembling hand to his father. "Read for yourself."

Daniel took the book gently from his hands and began to read.

Chapter 23

COLLECTING INTEL

*In order to end
You must have a beginning
Learn all that you can*

Ishmael stood inside the palace by the main entrance doors. His long, dark hair draped down the curves of his face framing the tight, square jaw line that was his most prominent feature. Ishmael was tall, but not to the height of Alder. He stood maybe four inches shorter at most. During the last Great War Ishmael was only a child. He was saved by Michael and Alder during a siege carried out by Evelyn and Azaroth. Found alone in the crumbled ruins of a destroyed courthouse, Alder and Michael took the boy in and Alder cared for him as if he was his own son.

A woman dressed in Caidel military armor stood next to him. She stood about five-foot eight and was voluptuous. She was in her late twenties and had dark, rose red hair that draped all the way down to her lower back. Sparks of red and orange gleamed off her silver armor. Instead of wearing leg plated armor a loose skirt hung from her waist. Her firm belief was that leg armor restricted movement to escape from enemies as a faster rate. As the leader of the Caidel military she was a highly regarded figure, indispensable to the kingdom. Her name was Scarlet.

"Scarlet, we've just been informed that Everworld is under attack by the Centrion Army," Ishmael said as he turned to face her.

"Figures," Scarlet replied as she rolled her blazing orange eyes. "I knew sooner or later something like this was coming. It's been far too quiet for far too long." She turned to face Ishmael. After a brief moment of silence both of them turned back to face Alder who stood before them, ready to give the pair a mission.

"Scarlet, what I ask of you and Ishmael is that you go collect intelligence regarding the whereabouts of the Centrion Army and the destruction they have caused to this point." He took a second to look into her eyes and saw the glimmer of understanding that spread like a wildfire in the night. "The faster this information can be discovered the better prepared we can be if they so choose to foolishly attack Caidel. I don't order but simply ask that you leave at once as time is currently not on our side."

Scarlet bobbed her head in a single nod, her lips pressed tightly together. "What happens if attack falls while we are away?"

"I shall take care of any invasion in your absence. I may not be the warrior I once was, and by no means am I the warrior you have proven yourself to be, time and time again, but the last thing I will do is let not only my kingdom down but those who believe in the power of its protectors."

To this Scarlet nodded and turned to face Ishmael who turned to face her. "We have a lot of ground to cover, so let us be off."

"Where do we begin?" Ishmael questioned.

"We set off to the Valley of Shadows," Scarlet firmly stated.

Ishmael nodded and knelt to one knee, then rose again.

Alder spoke up, "I wish you both the best and thank you for your service to Caidel. You may both be on your way." Both Ishmael and Scarlet nodded and turned, starting to walk away. "Oh, and Ishmael, whatever Scarlet asks of you, do it. I trust her with my life, and let me assure you, you can place your life in her hands as well." Alder smirked as neither Ishmael nor Scarlet turned back. Ishmael let out a single nod as he continued toward the castle doors, walking side-by-side with the most decorated and intelligent leader the Humanus Army has ever had.

As they exited through the castle doors the light of the stars poked through the blanket of darkness like never-dimming fireflies floating in the sky. They began their journey northwest toward the Valley of Shadows. As they reached the city boundaries a quiet shuffling sound rose. Scarlet reached to her hip where a lengthy sword was unleashed with the quickness of a lightning flash.

"General Scarlet," a modest voice spoke, "I mean you no harm." The voice seemed airy as if it were out of breath. "My name is Ferlone, son of Ferra. I ran as fast as I could to relay dreadful news: Asenfall has fallen to the Centrion Army. My dear friend and one of our most honorable generals, Poco, whispered but one word to me as he took his last breath. Can you guess what that word was? I'll tell you any-way, it was 'Caidel'. After he breathed his last breath I rushed here directly to talk to the prince to alert him of the Centrion and their invasion."

Scarlet sheathed her sword and spoke low and calm. "We have heard rumors of the Centrions leading attacks, and we are on our way to the Valley of Shadows to speak to the high chief as per plea of Prince Alder. Obtaining this validity of our beliefs we could turn back now," she paused. "Where are my manners? I'm sorry for the loss of your general and no doubt many of your kind."

"Thank you, General Scarlet," Ferlone said.

Ishmael broke in, "What are your orders, general?"

Scarlet closed her eyes in thought before opening them again and answered. "We carry on towards the Natarian Plains. We must know the size of the destructive path the Centrions have caused thus far."

"Aye," Ishmael responded.

"Ferlone, are you a warrior?" Scarlet's voice was soft, but piercing.

"Aye," he responded.

"Good. If we run into any trouble it's always nice to have an extra fighting hand at our side. I know not how you know my name, but I am grateful you do."

Ferlone nodded and all three set off and would walk for the next two hours until they came upon a dreadful sight.

The dark landscape painted a picture not quite as horrid as what truly happened. As the three descended into the Valley of Shadows corpses could be seen by the light of the stars strewn across the land. The fog had lifted and reflections of the stars could be seen in the pools of aqua blood. A group of small fires were positioned together which is where Scarlet led the others. They shambled and climbed over the mounds of bodies.

The firelight gleamed off her metal armor as Ahawi turned toward the direction of the sparks that flickered like a flame.

She lifted her bow but lowered it once she saw there were only three figures too small to be Centrions.

"My name is Scarlet Soto," her firm voice boomed out of the blackness. I am head general of Caidel's military. I've been sent on a mission to gather intelligence regarding rumors of the Centrions waging war. These two who accompany me are Ishmael Rasenbad of Caidel and Ferlone of Asenfall."

"My name is Ahawi Sahten. I am the head warrior of the Natarian people." She stood up to face Scarlet and both grasped each other's forearms in a form of mutual greeting.

Scarlet turned to see Chief Annikan rise. She fell to one knee and crossed her arm over her chest. "High Chief, I come seeking information."

"Please rise, Scarlet Soto of Caidel. I have heard many stories of the good deeds you have done and the accomplishments of your leadership. It is so good to see a friendly face on such a ferocious day. Today, many of our brothers and sisters were slain by the invading Centrions. If it were not for the leadership of Ahawi and the bravery of our elven brothers and sisters, the Natarian people may have ceased to exist on this very day."

Before Scarlet could answer Ezer rose to his feet and bent to one knee, crossing his arm over his chest and rose. "General Scarlet, I am Ezer Ingrid of Algernon. Today I lost not only a brother in arms, Feyler Bellin, but our queen, Evana, fell to a Centrion captain named Stoval. Stoval was then killed by Chief Annikan. Many have fallen today but the truth be known, Everworld is at war once again, there is no doubt."

"As you can see, general," Ahawi began, "our plains are stained in seas of blue and green. The attacking army is no more, but countless, innocent lives were lost today. We fought as one, as our numbers were too few to fight alone." Ahawi's final words came choked out.

"What are the prince's orders?" Annikan asked.

"That we strictly search for intelligence, but given the circumstance and the freedom of choice he allows me to make I suggest we all band together and head back to Caidel where further matters can be discussed as a counsel." All nodded. "Caidel has yet to be attacked and Asenfall is no more.

"Ferlone, what of your people?" Scarlet asked, already knowing the answer.

Ferlone described their near genocide at the hands of the Centrions. "Those who managed to escape I can only assume fled to Wickamore for hiding. We aren't on the best of terms with the gnomes but they are our closest allies. Our race will take a long time to recover from the destruction." Ferlone put his face in his hands and soft cries could be heard.

"Speaking of Wickamore, I wonder how the situation stands for the gnomes south in the forests?" Ahawi pondered.

"My best presumption given their sheer numbers and difficult terrain, any attempt to attack them is beyond foolish," Scarlet implied. "If I may be so bold, High Chief Annikan, I say gather all things necessary and come with us back to Caidel."

Annikan nodded. "You speak true and bold. Anyone Prince Alder gives full choice too I not only commend but I respect. We shall gather and be off at once."

Scarlet nodded in understanding. The exhausted Natarian and elven warriors gathered their belongings and began the long trek back to Caidel.

Chapter 24

THE BATTLE OF CAIDEL; THE BATTLE FOR EVERWORLD

And on this day those of greed will fall
The victory of the wicked is death
Black hearts turn to ash
As a sea of fire rains from the sky
Does death do you well?

Leaders, chiefs, generals and a prince, all capable of leading thousands into battle, and for better or for worse who would claim victory in the end, gathered together in the Grand Hall of the most beautiful castle in Everworld. A young girl named Mallory Bones accompanied these masters of war. Her father, a well-known figure in Everworld's history, helped stop a great war during his time there, and now she found herself in the midst of another. Thousands of civilians from all over Everworld took shelter inside the thick stone walls of Caidel as an army of Centrions, boar-like humanoid creatures hell bent on destruction, came from all directions closing in on the city. Not only was the fight for the capital at stake, but if Everworld were to survive the Centrions must be defeated.

Lee Odion, the head warrior of the Elven Army, spoke to another elven warrior named Ezer who had just survived an intense battle that took the life of Elven Queen Evana and Ezer's friend, second in command under Lee, Feyler Bellin. Upon hearing the news of the queen's murder and the corresponding death of his underling Feyler, Lee let out tears of sadness and choked back sobs as he fell to one knee and crossed his arm over his chest then placed his fist upon his forehead as a sign of respect for their deaths. Mallory had never seen Lee cry and this unnerved her.

Koel Lo'Hota, second in command of the Natarian people of the Valley of Shadows, rejoined his superior Ahawi Sahten and Chief Annikan Tawah. Koel was briefed on the battle that had taken place in his beloved homelands of the valley. He learned that the once beautiful green grasslands were now stained with the blood of his friends and enemies. He sat in silence and listened as his saddened eyes stared off into the distance. A few tears fell and he refused to wipe them away. The tears of a Natarian warrior were fuel; fuel that fed a fire of revenge.

The dwarf Ferlone stood alone. A sneak attack by the Centrions led to the virtual annihilation of his people. He watched as their general, Poco, fell to the hands of a Centrion captain named Luga. The health and whereabouts of their leader, Silverfang, remained unknown to those still alive, but Ferlone would be devastated to learn that he too had fallen at the hands of another Centrion captain named Daragorn. Poco's final word was "Caidel" as he drew his last breath, and Ferlone departed for the capital immediately under the blanket of smoke that hovered over his home of Asenfall. He turned back in horror to see it burning to the ground before racing away for good. The blazing orange fields became ash and the bright blue sky would never be the same blue that complemented it so well. Even the details of any citizens who escaped that terror were unknown.

However, the gnomes of Wickamore were far too many for two simple Centrion platoons to handle. A good majority of those platoons, led by the tired Daragorn and Luga, were lost that day – one sweet victory that came in a dire time of need. After the failed ambush, Daragorn and Luga retreated to gather new warriors and come back to fight fresh but that opportunity would never come about. The remnants of their platoons met with those of Gorga and Kaen whose sneak attack on Algernon was a bust as the elves got word of a possible attack and traveled to the Valley of Shadows to fight alongside their allies. This battle would result in a victory, but at a terrible cost. Many lives were lost that disastrous day in the Valley of Shadows, from both sides.

The Dark Queen Morgana who desired to rule over all of Everworld sat in her palace, the Castle of Shadows, mulling over the fact that her daughter had somehow mysteriously appeared in this world. She learned of her existence in Everworld only by the help of a wizard called – or by what he designated his own name to be – Crimson. The problem remained that Mallory believed her mother to be dead. She'd been missing from her life for so long, and for some random sorceress in a book she was transported into to claim to be her mother disgusted her to the core. Who was Mallory's mother anyway? She was a false mother who abandoned her and her father who was dying of cancer. At every attempt to persuade Mallory it truly was her, her daughter turned a blind eye. It was only after Mallory's meeting with Alder that she knew it truly was her mother after all.

Now, Mallory stood in the Grand Hall of Caidel Castle. Her mode of transportation into this world was in the hands of the Centrion's leader, Krum. Her mode of transportation out was in the hands of Prince Alder of Everworld. The only thing she had left was the Water of Tears that filled a vile hung around her neck like a necklace. This mysterious water holds the power to cure any disease, including the Final Death which on Earth is known as cancer. One way or another she would return to Earth and save her father's life; or she would die trying. He was all that she had left.

Prince Alder stood beside his right-hand man, Ishmael Rasenbad. He saw the other Great War come to an end with the help of Mallory's father, and he was determined to get her back home to save his life. Alder was also determined to save his people and all of Everworld. He knew nothing of Morgana's plans to take over, just as Morgana knew nothing of the Centrions' plan to take over after they succeeded and kill her so that it was only they who would rule. Ishmael would do whatever was asked of him by Alder, who, with Michael Bones, found him as a child at the end of the last Great War. Alder stood facing General Scarlet. Beauty, brains and brawn, she was not one to mess with and she was regarded by the prince himself as the best general the Humanus ever had. After their discussion, which was a recap of all the events leading up to their current situation, he approached Mallory and looked her in her crystal blue eyes.

"Mallory Bones, daughter of Michael Bones, war is coming to Caidel. There is no stopping it. I offer you this chance to go home now and cure your father. Leave our troubled world behind. You've been dragged into a war that you did not start and in a place you know very little about. Just say the word and I will have Ishmael fetch the book now." He waited patiently as Mallory stewed this thought over in her head.

Her heart yearned to go back to Earth and save her father. She didn't know how much time she had left, or if it was even too late already. He could be dead, not knowing where she went, thinking she had abandoned him as well. But deep down in her heart she knew that he knew where she was. She heard a voice at the Silver Lake when she was answering the riddles given to her by the lake guardian fairies. He was still alive, if just barely, but there was hope. After a small portion of time weighing the odds she responded: "No, I'm going to stay and fight this war with you. My father did and so shall I. If he were here he would see this through till the end and that's exactly what I plan on doing."

At this Alder smiled. His eyes squinted and he opened his mouth to speak. "You are just like your father – young and full of determination to do what's right, even in the face of danger with death being a serious possibility. Your father would be proud to know of this decision."

"Yes," she agreed, "I believe he's feeling that way right now." They smiled at each other.

"Stay close to Lee, he will be your guardian if the Centrion attack us here. He personally asked for this position and with his queen gone I granted him the duties he asked for. For now, I must gather all to summarize a plan that Scarlet and I have created to stop this war and bring peace back to our beautiful world."

Mallory ran to Lee's side and gripped his hand in hers and squeezed smiling up at him. "Guess you're stuck with me," she chortled.

"I would have it no other way. I vowed to keep you safe and get you home and that is what I plan to do." He smiled back at her and squeezed her hand once. Mallory watched closely as Alder walked up the staircase to the top landing overlooking the Grand Hall floor.

"Can I have everyone's attention, please?" Alder's voice was loud but not raised in anger or frustration. Every being in the room turned to face the prince of their beloved Everworld. "Today we expect to be attacked by creatures known as Centrions. These creatures are fierce and will stop at nothing to achieve victory. Many moons ago there was another Great War that ravaged Everworld. With the help of a man named Michael Bones, father to the young girl you see beside Lee Odion, that war came to an end and peace resumed upon our world. Today we fight for the same purpose. We fight for the longevity and peace of this world we call home. Now, prepare yourselves. Warriors of all races gather under your leaders and trust their battle abilities and intelligence. Though we fight alongside our brothers of the same race we also fight as one worldly family. We either live together, or die together." There was a short pause as Alder looked upon all, their eyes glued to him. "Families and civilians will be placed inside the palace's cellar. There is only one entrance and it is hidden. Only two people know the entrance and both would as soon die as give up its location. However, one must stay there to make sure the civilians get out once we have won in case the other falls. We will win this war and Everworld will be at peace forevermore."

Mallory let go of Lee's hand and walked forward. Everyone else stood still. She stopped after a couple steps and looked up at Alder. "Prince Alder, I am no warrior, but I refuse to cower and hide in the cellars," her voice echoed in the silent hall. "I will fight alongside you, whether it means life or death."

Prince Alder stood still for a moment and nodded. "Out of respect for your father, and a growing respect for you," he smiled, "whatever your strengths may be I ask that you perform them to the best of your abilities."

"You can count on me!" She nodded and walked back to Lee's side.

"Ishmael," Alder turned toward his right-hand man and continued, "I ask that you guide all civilians toward the one who knows the cellars and then proceed to meet me back here." Ishmael nodded.

Alder turned back toward the crowd. "Your battle stations and posts will now be set so please listen carefully. There are many more of them than there are of us, so strategy is very important. Confer with your commanders to determine precise post locations. Elven warriors please follow under the direction of Ahawi Sahten, head warrior of the Natarians. Natarian and elven warriors will be scattered within and on top of the city walls." He spread his arms for physical clarification. "Those who carry bows will be perched above with some hiding within the tower windows. Those who carry swords or other melee weapons will be soldiers on the ground and will engage in hand-to-hand combat." He brought his hand together in close-fingered prayer. He unlaced his fingers and clenched his hands into tight fists and looked down upon them. "Remember," he spoke looking down, relaxing his hands and raising his head, "these creatures are very strong. Trying to overpower them is pointless. Be nimble, be quick. Speed will be your ally. Now go, my friends and allies, and get situated. They will arrive before we know it. Time is also our enemy." All proceeded to leave the Great Hall. "Koel, Lee and Mallory, I ask you join me up here." The trio proceeded up the stairs as the hall emptied out.

"Yes, Prince Alder?" Lee's voice was soft.

"You, Koel, Mallory, Scarlet and I will fight within the castle shall it be entered. Koel, Ishmael and I will be on the floor below. Mallory and Lee stay above. Someone special will be joining you." They all nodded, even Lee and Mallory who both looked confused. "Pray we for victory," Alder concluded. "Pray we for life."

Michael Bones, using what remained of his strength, sat up in bed and coughed hard. Blood spat out into the napkin he placed over his mouth. Without looking he closed the napkin and tossed it into the bin near his bedside.

"What's the good news, dad?" Michael asked and laughed at his horrible attempt at a mood lightener.

"The battle for Caidel is set to unfold, Michael. Mallory refuses to hide. She demanded to fight and Alder accepted." He looked up, alarmed, but only saw Michael smiling.

"That's my girl." He smiled and took a sip of the coffee Daniel had set upon his bedside table for him. "Oh, and I ask one thing."

"What's that, son?"

"Read to me every event as it unfolds. No matter how bad it gets I need to know." Daniel nodded and read aloud as the words appeared like magic.

"Gray skies shadowed an already dreary feeling that lived inside every single soldier that stood to defend Caidel..." he began.

On a more positive note there was no fog. The air was clear but the sky was covered. The beautiful city walls were decorated with intricacies carved into its beautiful stone base. Standing on top of archways and pillars stood archers of the Natarian race from the Valley of Shadows and elven warriors from the city of Algernon. Standing below on the streets of Caidel, soon to be shaken by battle, were the men and women whose abilities to do battle with swords, axes and other melee objects of war, were their strengths. Wind, invisible like time, whistled through the otherwise silent air.

The wind was soon drowned in an audible blast that echoed over the skies and through the winding streets where warriors sat in patience and in fear. They were coming. The Centrions were coming and that was made crystal clear by the battle call of the horn that broke the whispering silence.

To the west of Caidel were hills that gave options for two paths. One that led to the Muddy Hills, were these despicable creatures who wanted to claim Everworld were from, and one that lead to Algernon, a city that shocked the Centrion troops as it was found to be vacant at the time of their attack.

To the east of Caidel was East Bay, where swashbucklers and fishermen spent their days, and Morningshire, a ghostly shell of a city left in shambles after the last Great War. Only a few elven scouts who stood inside the east towers faced in that direction in case of a cowardly sneak attack. The scouts high in the towers could alert the warriors below so reinforcements could arrive before the Centrions even came close to the city walls.

Ezer, the elven warrior still mourning the loss of his queen, stood on top of the front walls facing west. He held his sword up high over his head.

"The enemy approaches!" He screamed the words so the entire kingdom could hear his cry. "Warriors of the bow take aim and aim your arrows high. On my mark light them on fire with the torches provided and on my command release them. The enemy shall see an inferno rain down upon them like stars falling from the skies." The strength in his voice boomed each sentence like the Centrions battle horn. He continued: "General and head warrior Ahawi Sahten of the Natarian warriors will guide us — to all, trust her with your life, for some of us will die, but for the sake of Everworld's future we must fight. I leave you with this: This is our home, now protect it!"

The grounds began to tremble beneath their feet. Ahawi stood on top of the wall nearest the front door to the palace. Chief Annikan stood beside her.

"Ahawi," Annikan said facing the woman who had led the warriors of his people and kept their land safe. "Knaht ouy, rof gniht y-reve. Yo duorp ot lac ouy ylimaf."

Ahawi smiled. "Dna yo duorp ot lac ouy yo rehtaf." A tear fell from Annikan's cheek as they both turned back preparing for the fight of their lives.

The quakes grew stronger and over the rolling hills to the west came a mass of beasts. There were almost five-hundred in number. These boar-like men with tusks and beady black eyes held swords in one enormous hand and shields made from the densest wood in all of Everworld, Blackwood, in the other. Leading the charge was Krum, the absolute head general of the Centrion Army. Behind him marched generals Drayt and Gilf who led four Centrions, all captains of the Centrion Army, behind them. Luga, pound-for-pound the strongest of all the Centrions marched from the left. Second to left marched Daragorn, the newest Centrion captain with the least amount of experience. Luga and Daragorn swiftly conquered Asenfall but their attempts to take out Wickamore backfired. Second to the right marched Gorga, the most intelligent of the captains. His big nose made him easily identifiable. Finally, all the way to the right, with a look of pure evil on his face marched Kaen. Kaen was wicked. Like Gorga he had an identifiable mark, a scar from a slash just below his left eye that he received in the last Great War. He was the youngest captain back then, scared and inexperienced. He was now the most ruthless, not caring who he had to kill to survive and succeed, even his own men. The fifth and sixth captains of the Centrion Army were no longer with them. Those captains, Stoval and Dragu, had fallen at the hands of Chief Annikan and the Natarian army's general, Ahawi Sahten. Behind the four remaining captains was a massive sea of monsters.

Krum halted and raised his fist high in the air. The point of his enormous sword in his right hand pointed to the dull-gray heavens. The massive shield strapped to his left arm hung by his side. Krum, Drayt, Gilf, Kaen, Gorga, Luga, and Daragorn looked ahead and saw the mass of soldiers lined on the walls of Caidel.

"Nock and light your arrows!" Ezer screamed.

Like motionless fireflies little dots of light pock-marked the air.

"Raise your shields above your heads!" The demand by Krum echoed over the hills where the Centrion soldiers came to rest. Like a wave the shields went up line by line. "Ready men?" he questioned. "This world will be ours!" A promise he intended to keep escaped his lips. A roar of approval and belief swam up from the sea of bodies below him. "Our wives and our children will grow up in a world which accepts our kind. No more shall we be confined to the Muddy Hills. The beauty of this world will be all ours to rule over. Stoval and Dragu have fallen, but we all remain." Another round of roaring followed. "Gorga, do the honors."

Gorga raised his sword and yelled the battle cry of his platoon, "Ferlaugh!"

"Ferlaugh," the war cry was mimicked by his platoon and after by all other platoons.

Krum lowered his sword as Drayt, Gilf, and all the captains ran past him. Wave upon wave of Centrion followed. A glint of evil shimmered in Krum's eyes.

"Now!" Ezer commanded. The motionless firefly lights came to life and rose into the air with tremendous speed. They arched like a rainbow as a firestorm rained down like hail onto the shield-covered Centrions. A plethora of arrows stuck out on shields, slowly setting them on fire. The scene imitated a moving forest of sapling twigs. The Centrion soldiers slowed as they funneled into entrances of the city walls.

Inside the walls bodies began to clash, swords clanged together and deep thunking sounds reverberated as swords cut into shields. From the top of the city walls arrows flew like missiles hitting their targets left and right. The tough skin mixed with the armor of the Centrions rejected and reflected most arrows but the constant feel of what felt like pebbles being thrown at them was enough to distract them. As Centrions were turning to growl and grunt skilled swordsmen and women plunged their weapons between the cracks of armor wherever they could. The neck and eyes made perfect spots of deadly entry.

As more Centrions funneled in it gave Daragorn and Luga a chance to escape the heat of battle and work their way towards the palace gates. This was the task set for all the captains and generals while the other soldiers cleaned up behind them. Daragorn and Luga moved swiftly, blocking any sword attacks with their giant shields and kept their heads down low to prevent any arrows finding their way into their eyes or noses. After what equated to running through a maze they came across a stairway that lead them up onto the walls. An elven soldier named Peltra with pink eyes was first to greet the Centrion captains but her arrows only bounced off. She reached down quickly for her dagger and threw it like a throwing knife but Daragorn slapped it out of the air with his shield.

"Sorry little elven girl," he laughed. His gruff voice made her recoil. "That's not good enough." He swung his shield into her side, the force crushing her ribs into her stomach and smashing her face in as she fell from the wall to the ground with a thud. Others also tried to stop them but all were dispatched with ease.

Luga let out a growl as he dropped his sword and reached up to a spot just between his shoulder and neck. An arrow jutted from the crack. He pulled it out and turned to see Ahawi and Annikan atop the wall nearest to the palace entrance.

"Look over there," Luga stated. "That Natarian female scum just shot me. She's mine. You deal with the chief. Someone killed off Dragu and Stoval and I reckon it was them. I don't care about those two. Their idiocy got them killed. If they did it, it means they're tough, and I love a challenge."

"Luga," Daragorn said, "Annikan is physically stronger than her. You are the strongest of all Centrions. I know she shot you but its better if you take on the chief.

"Yes, I see your point," Luga agreed. Both Centrion captains proceeded towards the defenders of Everworld. Their shields and swords fended off each arrow that Annikan and Ahawi sent their way eventually coming within striking distance.

Ahawi dropped her bow and drew a sword she had equipped specifically for this battle. She knew her strength was in her bow but she came prepared to fight. She slashed at Daragorn, the sound of steel clanged together. Being more familiar and skilled with a sword he waited for her to slash and knocked it away before throwing his shield at her, knocking her off the wall to the ground below. He jumped down after her. Luga and Annikan stood eye-to-eye.

Behind a hole in the wall on the ground sat Ferlone. Patiently he waited for a moment to attack. Ahawi was slowly standing up as Daragorn walked over to her with a cocky stride. He dropped his sword and cocked his fist before rocketing it into her face. She stumbled backward and fell, spitting out the blue blood that was unique to the Natarian race. He hit her again as she stumbled to stay upright. She counted two right hands and now expected him to swing his shield with his left. He did as predicted and she ducked under and behind him. He stumbled forward from the force of the swing. When he turned around the battered woman he expected to be there was replaced by a small, red creature with a thick silver sword made from Algerite, the strongest metal in all of Everworld and crafted in Asenfall. Daragorn had no chance to make a move before the sword was plunged deep into his exposed throat. Green blood spat from his throat before Ferlone pulled it free. Daragorn swung his shield frantically to try to hit the shifty dwarf who dodged with ease before watching the beast fall to his knees, then ultimately the ground. Daragorn choked on his own blood as his last gasps escaped from his lips. Ferlone wiped the green goo onto his sleeve and dropped the sword. He ran over to Ahawi who had run and hid as part of a backup plan which succeeded.

"General Ahawi, are you alright?" The voice of the dwarf was shaky.

"I'm fine, just beaten and bruised," she paused. "Ferlone thank you for saving my life. I owe you the greatest debt of gratitude."

"You owe me nothing, miss. We fight this war together. Let us heal your wounds."

"No, I fight till the battle is over." She picked up her sword which lay a few feet from Daragorn's corpse. "Come with me. More captains will be coming and we can't take them all, but inside the Grand Hall of the palace await other soldiers who can." She spat blood onto the ground. "For now we fight alongside our brothers and sisters." The pair began to set off back through the entrance Luga and Daragorn came through until she heard a thud.

Atop the wall from which Ahawi was knocked Luga and Annikan began to fight. Annikan dodged every slash of the sword and swing of the shield. He allowed Luga to get close and swiftly slide his sword along Luga's arm and cut the straps to his shield. The shield fell. Without batting an eye Luga took the opportunity to seize Annikan by the throat. He ripped the sword from the chief's hands and began to squeeze. Annikan wheezed before Luga slammed him down. His body lay, spread across the top of the wall. Luga kicked him off to the ground below. Annikan reached for his throat, unable to breathe. Luga jumped down and stood over Annikan. As he looked down into his eyes Ahawi and Ferlone started to run back.

"Annikan!" Ahawi screamed. "No!"

Without flinching Luga drew his sword high into the air. "Goodnight, Annikan. Your people are now mine!" He thrust the sword down into the heart of the Natarian High Chief. Blood flew up like a fountain from Annikan's mouth. Ahawi screamed and rushed at Luga who swung his arm out and threw her aside. She tumbled to the ground. She crawled backward as Luga moved forward with his sword raised. Just as he began to swing he felt a heavy thud against his back that sent him sprawling forward. He landed on his face and turned over ready to get up, but before he could Ferlone jumped on top of him and placed the point of his Algerite sword against his neck.

"You own no one, but you owe death." Ferlone spoke these words as he slid the sword across the exposed neck of Luga. Luga was dead instantly. He wiped the green blood off the sword on his other sleeve.

Ahawi ran over to the dead body of her chief and knelt next to him. She tried to concentrate but all the sounds of screams and torture buzzed the air with a frequency loud enough to blanket thoughts. Her mind raced seemingly to nowhere. Ferlone came to her side and put his hand on her shoulder.

"Now is no time to mourn. They need our help out there."

Ahawi turned to Ferlone, her eyes filled with tears that overflowed and sprinkled the ground below. She nodded and got to her feet. She closed her eyes. When she opened her eyes instead of water there was fire. Her determination had never been so high. The pair set off running into the thick of an all-out war.

Drayt, Gilf, Gorga and Kaen moved swiftly through the crowded battle site and found their way to the front door of the palace.

"How do you propose we enter?" Gilf's strong Irish tone sarcastically demanded.

"We could…" Drayt's deep voice began.

"You could move," the calm voice of Kaen spoke and he pushed past them to the door. Kaen kicked the door which rattled on its hinges but didn't break.

"Kaen I don't think…" Gorga started.

Bang!

"Kaen this won't…" He tried again.

Bang!

"Whatever." He said.

Bang! After the fourth kick the locks on the door broke and gave way. The door to the palace swung open. The two generals and Gorga looked in disbelief, their mouths hung open.

Kaen led the way inside where an arrow came whizzing directly towards his left eye. He snatched the arrow in his fingers inches from it. "I'm scarred, not blind," he said coldly before snapping the arrow between his thumb, forefinger and middle finger. The four Centrions stood just inside the door to the Grand Hall. Mallory, Lee, Koel, Scarlet and Alder stood on the other side of it.

Moments after Kaen snapped the arrow like a twig Ishmael came running and stopped next to Alder. Everyone had safely been locked into the cellar.

"I want the Natarian," Drayt said.

"The prince is mine," the cold voice of Kaen said.

The Centrions started forward before an explosion of black smoke filled the hall. Lee nocked his bow. Koel, Alder and Ishmael drew their swords. As the smoke began to dissipate a female figure began to form.

Morgana stepped out from the remainder of the smoke facing the Centrions. She smiled at them and turned around to face Mallory. She held her hands up to show she had no evil intention and slowly walked over to Mallory looking at everyone as she did so. "Mallory, May I please speak to you?"

"You say you are truly my mother," Mallory said. "What more is there to say?"

"I want to prove to you I am her. I wish to fight alongside you against these despicable creatures."

"Despicable?" Ishmael spat. "You're one to talk."

"I have done much wrong and many things I will forever be ashamed of, but I'm willing to do anything to have Mallory back in my life."

"I don't trust her," Ishmael said to Alder.

"I don't trust her either," Alder agreed.

"And why should we?" questioned Ishmael.

Morgana turned to face the Centrions. She lowered her arms to her side and raised her right. She spoke one word, "Pyrebust." A small, red, glowing orb shot out of her hand and sped toward Drayt with no time for him to react. The orb entered his body and the sound of fire crackling began as he burst into flames. He was burning alive but his heart had already burst. His body fell to its knees and quickly toppled onto its front. The flames continued until only charred remains were left. The other Centrions looked on in horror.

"I'm sorry you had to see that Mallory but I had to make the most impactful point I possibly could. These creatures are here to kill you and everyone else, and I will do whatever I must to protect you." She turned around to face Mallory before saying, "Please believe me. I'm here to help you and end this war. I wish to be wicked no more."

"I lied," Ishmael scoffed. "It's definitely better we have her on our side."

"One false move and I kill you where you stand," said Alder. "It's also my duty and honor to protect Mallory Bones. Just remember that," he finished.

"Understood," Morgana agreed, staring into his eyes.

"Of course you'd be here." Another Centrion entered the room and closed the broken door behind him. "I'm glad we had a secret plan to kill you off after the war." Krum stood in front of the locked door. His weapon he called "Warhammer" swung by his side. The leather strap attached to the end keeping it tied to his wrist.

Morgana's eyes squinted. "We are both filthy creatures, but only one can survive. Let me begin my journey to forgiveness by disposing of one who would never ask for it."

The silence broke as Gilf roared in anger at the death of his fellow general and made a charge directly at Morgana but was cut off by Scarlet.

Gorga began to ascend the staircase as Lee shot multiple arrows from above.

Kaen made a direct charge at Alder but Mallory jumped down in front of him.

Krum raised his Warhammer and Morgana raised her arms. Krum's shield deflected all spells she threw at him.

"Why are they being repelled?" she asked.

Krum laughed. "You can thank Azaroth for the protection. At the end of the Great War he enchanted it for me. We've planned for this a long time, Morgana. You have absolutely no idea."

Gilf's rage blinded his ability to fight and Scarlet knocked him to the floor. She then saw Mallory leap in front of Alder as Kaen approached and ran to attack him. As she stabbed Kaen in the thigh he grunted and turned around. The rose-headed general tried to pull the knife from his thigh but the skin was too thick and the blade became stuck. Kaen swung his sword halfway over Scarlet's head. Scarlet instinctively ducked and dodged backwards. Koel took the opportunity to lung at Kaen but with his natural ability to fight his knee rose like lightning and nailed him in the chest cracking four of his ribs. Koel gasped as droplets of blue fell to the floor.

"Koel!" Mallory cried and tried to run to him but Alder held her back. Ishmael ran to attack the Centrion beast but Kaen sensed him coming. He threw Ishmael to the ground and picked up the wounded warrior dripping blood. His hand clasped around Koel's mouth. The grip was so tight Koel couldn't open his mouth to scream or fight and the pain was too unbearable to try to swing his arms or legs to fight.

"One less pest," Kaen said coldly before plunging his sword through the heart of the brave warrior.

"No!" Mallory screamed as tears strolled down her cheeks. "Koel, no! No! No! No!" She screamed in rage as her tears continued to fall.

"You shall die for this, Centrion." Scarlet said with gritted teeth and lunged back at the Kaen. The two clashed together and began to duel once more.

As Koel lay dying on the floor, Lee knew his bow wouldn't be of use if Gorga got too close so he dropped it and pulled out his sword. The two battled back and forth. The strength of the Centrion soon became too much and Lee began to run out of options. He eyed the edge of the balcony and set his back to it. Gorga pushed Lee against it.

"What now, elf? I've got you cornered and in my grip. You can't get behind me to push or kick me over."

Lee just smiled at him and laughed. "You thought that was my plan? While it makes sense I'm more intelligent than that. I'm more intelligent than you. If you're the smartest the Centrion have to offer this battle is already over."

"What do you mean?" Gorga spat in anger.

"Mallory, I promised to get you home any way I could," Lee said.

"Lee what do you …" Mallory began.

"When you get back and cure your father let him know I'll forever be grateful for what he did for our world.

"I don't understand," she said frustrated.

Lee closed his eyes and gripped Gorga tightly.

"Hey, what are you doing?" Gorga cracked.

Lee leaned his body over the railing to tumble backwards, taking Gorga with him.

"Lee, no!" Mallory screamed out in an ear-piercing shriek.

Only one thud could be heard. Lee's body levitated inches from the floor. Gorga lay on the ground as green blood seeped out of his crushed skull. Mallory watched in awe as Lee levitated back up to the balcony and was met by a figure in white.

Mallory stood frozen in place. Alder looked up and smiled.

"Azarim, you sure know how to make an entrance."

"Azarim?" Mallory exclaimed. "The wizard from the stories?"

"Yes, and you must be young Mallory Bones." He snapped his fingers and Mallory appeared on top of the balcony by Lee's side. Lee was still in shock from his near-death experience and his knees gave way as he fell to the ground.

"Thank you, great wizard," Lee managed to get out still trying to breathe.

"No need to thank…" Azarim's words were cut short as his heart appeared in front of his chest. A black mist began to surround him dowsing the light as the light in his eyes faded to glass. He fell to the floor with a thud. A red heart sat in the palm of a figure cloaked in black. A hood covered his face. The heart beat a few more times before it turned into a dark purple mist that vanished into dust and became sucked into the cloaked body of this figure.

The figure turned toward Mallory. It seemed to happen in slow motion. It raised its arm and a black beam shot out and struck into Mallory's heart. Morgana screamed and became paralyzed as she was thrown across the room. The cloaked figure turned toward Lee whose eyes were wide with terror.

The figure in black turned his head quickly away and disappeared moments before a blast echoed on the balcony.

"Mallory!" screamed Alder.

Morgana watched in horror as electrical smoke spun in a cloud of dust. As the dust evaporated a clear protective shield was covering

Mallory and Lee. A figure clad in gray walked over to them. The red eyes looked down upon them.

"Heal her," Crimson said. "Now! Use the Water of Tears!" he demanded. "She must live!" Lee reached for the vile, pulled it out of Mallory's shirt and opened it. Mallory's breathing began to slow and her eyes began to turn to glass. The liquid dripped down her throat and ever so slowly the hole in her chest and heart began to reverse and heal. Her eyes came alive with fluid and she gasped for air. Slowly her breathing returned to normal.

"What happened?" she asked. She looked down to see the vile outside of her shirt and empty. "No! Not the water." Her breathing quickened as she began to panic. "My dad. My dad is going to die! Why did you use the water on me? Why did you use the water on me!" she screamed.

"Because," Crimson spoke. Mallory turned to see the sorcerer in gray.

"C-Crimson?" Mallory asked?

Crimson looked over the balcony to where Krum stood over Morgana. Krum lifted his sword and Mallory's eyes widened with terror as she saw him bring the sword down towards Morgana. Krum was thrown aside violently, his sword flying from his hand as he collided with the wall. He then turned toward Kaen. His eyes turned blood red and glowed like a fire at midnight. Krum grabbed his chest. Scarlet stood back unsure of what was happening. His lungs were collapsing in upon themselves. Crimson was squeezing his lungs from the inside. A whirlwind of electricity began to fly around Kaen.

"Lee, this one is your kill," Crimson said.

Lee nodded. He strapped his quiver of arrows over his shoulder and made his way to where Kaen hovered, gasping for air. Lee looked into his eyes.

"For my brother Koel, I'll see you in hell." He pulled an arrow out from his quiver and spun it in his hand, arrow pointing down. He slammed it down through the Centrions armor and into his heart. Lee let go of the arrow and Kaen fell to the floor, dead.

Alder walked over to Krum. Krum stumbled in an attempt to get up and looked into the eyes of Alder.

"Please, let me live. All I wanted was the best for my people," Krum pleaded as he grabbed the shirt of Alder in supplication.

"Let you live when your desire was mass genocide? Why the hell should I let you live?"

"Your majesty," a small, humble voice spoke from the crowd. "Please do not kill him. Lock him away for life, but he's not worth the blood on your hands."

Alder looked back to see Mallory looking at him with her hands crossed in front of her. He looked back into the eyes of Krum and sighed.

"You live because Mallory Bones allows it."

"Thank you, thank you," Krum started but before he could continue he was set on fire just like Drayt and he burned and burned until only ash was left.

Morgana – having been freed from her paralysis when the cloaked figure left – caught the eyes of Mallory who looked at her in horror and disgust. "Mallory it wasn't me, I swear."

"It was me," Crimson spoke.

"But why," Mallory asked. "I'm so tired of death."

"The reason is far too difficult to explain, but your future depends on his death." She stared up at him, confused and questioning. "Death is a part of life," he continued, "you will find out why. I can't say when or where, but you will."

"Crimson, is it?" Alder spoke up. "I thank you, gray wizard but who sent for you?"

"Azarim and I made this plan in secret. Sadly, Azaroth got away before I could kill him but Azarim knows my power probably wouldn't have been enough to finish him off anyways." My duty is to keep building my power and find Azaroth to finish him once and for all."

Mallory looked back down at the empty vile and tears began to fall again. "Daddy," she said out loud. "Daddy I'm so sorry." She wept into her hands for a very long time.

Back on Earth Michael closed his eyes and coughed. He laughed. Daniel looked over at him, tears streamed down his face.

"Why do you laugh?" Daniel asked. "Your daughter risked her life to save you and now her one chance is gone."

"I could never be more proud of the daughter that I have raised. She did all of this for me and at the same time it seems that she's converted her mother back into her mother again." He coughed and spat up phlegm mixed with blood into his tissue. "While my death for her will be a struggle, it shows her that you can't save everyone. Not every story in life has a happy ending. She will eventually be okay."

Daniel wiped the tears from his eyes. "Do you really think my daughter will come back and be her mother again?"

"Without a doubt," Michael answered. "We can talk when Mallory gets back. No matter what I'm holding on until then. Please keep reading to me Daniel. I need to know if my little girl stays safe."

Daniel nodded and continued to read.

Chapter 25

THE AFTERMATH

The war is over now, It's okay to cry
Sometimes some bad guys win
Sometimes some good guys die

But every war will have an end
And only the best succeed
Unchained by the crooked few
From the land that they have freed

Prince Alder and Crimson climbed to the top of the highest tower. Alder looked out upon the war that continued to wage below. On the wall of the tower room was a horn. He took it off the wall and proceeded to the window where he blew it hard. It had no effect. The clashing of swords and cries of the dying were far too great. He tried again to no avail.

"Come here," Crimson said. Weary of his intentions, Alder stayed put. "Come here," Crimson repeated and waved his hand in a 'come to me' motion. Slowly Alder walked over and Crimson slowly raised his index and middle fingers to Alder's neck. A light blue aura glowed for a moment before it vanished.

"What did you do to me?" Alder asked as he touched his neck where Crimson's fingers had caressed.

"Go, speak to the masses. Tell the Centrions the war is over and they have lost."

Alder walked over to the window and tried to speak. Instead of the normal volume and tone his voice held, it had amplified significantly. "Listen to me, for I am Prince Alder of Caidel." The sound of his voice almost muted the sounds of the battles below.

On the grounds of Caidel the fighting slowly came to a stop as all turned to see where this seeming voice of God was coming from.

"I'm at the top of the west tower. I call to all Centrions and pray you listen. This war is over. Your captains and leaders have all been killed. If you stop now I will command all soldiers to let you leave in peace. If you continue to fight, all soldiers will be captured or killed." Grunts of disbelief filled the air.

"Why should we believe you?" A scruffy Centrion's voice cried from down below.

"Let this Centrion pass and allow him in to the tower to see the proof he seeks. Make way for him and do him no harm." The Centrion walked over fallen corpses, a small graveyard for the newly slain. He walked through puddles of multi-colored blood until he reached the entrance doors to the palace and stepped inside. Alder continued: "Cease all action until he returns with the truth I have already exposed. While this war has been declared over, Centrions will be free to go home, at least those who remain alive. Your kind shall be watched closely from now on until proof of coexistence reveals itself to the fullest." He turned to Crimson who nodded back at him.

Down below in the Grand Hall Lee consoled Mallory. Morgana crept closer unsure of what to do, what to say. Mallory looked at her unsure of her own actions.

"Mallory, I have no words. I ask, no, I beg that you give me a chance to return and be the mother I should have been a long time ago."

"And what about my father?" she cut her off demanding. "He will surely die unless you know some spell to cure his cancer."

Morgana looked distressingly as her daughter still sobbed. "There is no spell for that, my daughter. Only the Water of Tears can save him."

"But I can't go back," Mallory said. "I can't go back."

"No," Morgana agreed. "I'm sorry."

The room sat silent for a second until Alder's voice was heard from above them. He stood on the balcony near the entrance to the west tower. At the same time the front door opened and in stepped a Centrion. Everyone readied their weapon but Alder spoke out calmly. "Do him no harm. He is here to bear witness to the end of this war. All Centrions are allowed to leave and return home, but their civilization shall be kept under surveillance until they can prove they will no longer be a war-mongering race."

The Centrion looked around at his fallen leaders and his eyes fell upon the body of Kaen. He sighed and dropped to his knees dropping his weapon in the process.

"Rise and tell the others. It's time to clean up the damage this war has caused. Leave and think about what you've witnessed here today and maybe lead them away from anger."

"Yes, sir," the Centrion said. In obvious shame he began to walk away. "I wish to pay my repentance with my life," he spoke.

"No," Mallory's voice was sharp and clear. "No more killing, I'm so tired of all the killing. Just leave and change. Grow and become better creatures, better people. Everyone deserves a second chance." She paused for a moment before turning back to Morgana. "Everyone deserves a second chance," she softly repeated. She walked over to her mother and grabbed her hands and looked up into her eyes.

"Morgana," she said, "it's time for you to come home. It's time for us to go home. Oh," she continued, "and it's going to take time for me to start calling you mom again, that better be clearly understood."

"I understand," Morgana said. She took Mallory into her arms and hugged her close. Reluctantly, Mallory crossed her arms over her mother's back.

The Centrion exited through the door to tell the others of this truth. The war was over and the clean-up began.

"Ishmael," Alder said as the door shut behind the lost solider, go grab the book. After a few days of rest and recovery we will send these two home." Ishmael gave the sign of respect and walked away. "Oh!" Alder yelled after him, "and don't forget to release the civilians from the cellar. Let them know the war is over and victory has been claimed. Warn them about the destruction they will witness." He walked over to Lee and shook his hand. "Lee Odion, your service and fearlessness will never be forgotten. Thank you for the courage you have shown here today." Lee looked into his eyes and nodded. He walked over to Crimson. "Crimson," he said, "thank you for choosing the right side to fight for. Azarim would be proud." Crimson bowed in respect. "Mallory and Morgana, thank you both for everything you did here today." He walked over to Scarlet and crossed his arm over his chest. "Thank you, general." Finally, he walked over to the fallen body of the Natarian warrior. All eyes were on Alder and a sad silence hung in the air. "Koel Lo'Hota, you, my fallen friend, my fallen brother, will never be forgotten. Your name shall reign in history for the sacrifice and bravery you showed here today. A ceremony shall be held in your honor and in honor of those who have fallen as well. Let us now leave. More sadness awaits outside."

Upon exit of the palace doors three bodies lay on the ground. Two were of Centrion captains and the other, that of Annikan Tawah. Two pairs of footsteps were heard rushing in their direction but nobody prepared for any sort of battle. A few seconds later Ahawi and Ferlone turned the corner.

All were now gathered around the soulless chief. Ahawi dropped down slowly to her knees, bent over him, and prayed. She stood up and turned toward Alder. They looked at each other in silence. Alder nodded first, then Ahawi. "The child with the sapphire eyes," she said.

"Yes," Alder agreed. "Unfortunately, I bear more bad news."

Ahawi clenched her fists and looked back and forth between his eyes. "What is it Prince Alder?"

"Koel Lo'Hota sacrificed himself inside during the fight. He has passed on. His spirit now watches over you and all the Natarian people." A single tear slid down her face. These tears would number far greater later on through the night. "Come," he said. "There is much work to do."

Ferlone tagged along as he knew not of the whereabouts of his race. "Prince Alder," he said, "what of my people?"

The Prince gazed at him sadly. "I do not know, therefore I cannot say. I will send some warriors with you to help search for them. I only hope and pray that some made it out alive and took residence in either the hobbles of Morningshire or found refuge amongst the gnomes. Your race is most close with theirs if I remember correctly."

"Thank you, your majesty," Ferlone replied as he walked with them toward the city entrance.

All Centrions dropped their weapons and shields one by one as the forlorn Centrion, who had been allowed inside, walked past them with a blank gaze and no weapons. Each Centrion he passed fell in behind him in a line as he walked them out of the battlefield and back to the mountains where he would address them that a new world was beginning for them. No longer would they be a people of war, but one of peace.

As the day faded to night people from every race came up from the underground to see the carnage of the war. Some cried in disgust, some in sadness and some in rage. Over the next few days the streets would be cleaned up and bodies disposed of, but the notice of destruction never forgotten.

Chapter 26

A NEW KING, A NEW CHIEF, A NEW DAY

A warrior now crowned a king
In honor of his mighty deeds
He serves the people not himself
His humble, tired, war-torn self

A child so different than the rest
Was birthed to bear a royal crest
He'll learn the ways and lead his kind
Through humble heart and open mind

But after war what's there is left
A fresh new life, an air of breath
Begin anew and you will see
The change begins with you and me

The Valley of Shadows still hadn't fully recovered even after all the bodies had finally been wrapped and buried, or burned if disease had begun to cast its shadow. Survivors of Asenfall had been found hiding both within the shamble of Morningshire and in the woods of Wickamore.

The Village of Algernon was spared by the elves decision to fight alongside their brothers in the Valley of Shadows. One big ceremony was being held for all. A crowning of a new king and that of a new high chief were set to take place. Standing on top of the base of a water fountain inscribed with the initials M.B., Alder spoke to a gathering that completely filled the opening within the center of the village. To his left, standing on the ground just in front of the fountain and holding a beautiful new long, feathered crown was Ahawi, and to his right, Ishmael, who held a beautiful crown made from pearls and diamonds woven together.

"Today marks three new beginnings for Everworld." He looked out over the masses, turning to see all as he spoke. "Sadly, during the war, two great leaders of two of our great nations passed on from this world. Their spirits watch over us all today as we celebrate a new life and a birthing of new leaders who will lead their people on to greatness. I ask at this moment that Lee Odion step forward." Lee stepped forward and knelt before Prince Alder, clenched his fist and lifted it to his forehead. "Next, there is a young man who questions his existence in this world. Long ago a prophecy told of a young child who would bear eyes the color of sapphire. The child was born, fittingly, to Head Warrior Ahawi Sahten. His name is Tokano and I ask that he step forward at this time." The young child was only ten years old but he bravely stepped forward.

"Don't be afraid, my son." Ahawi smiled at him and he took his place in front of her.

"It is said that after the child bearing sapphire eyes is born and when he attains the age of ten years that new change would be taking place. That prophecy seems to have come true. Although Tokano may be young he will be taught the ways and I have no doubt he will have his mother's intelligence and learn with ease."

Mallory Bones stood between the two new leaders.

"I ask Mallory Bones to also come forward at this time." She stepped forward nervously, blushing ever so slightly. "Your importance is far greater than you understand. You were able to change someone's heart, and that is a rare feat for anyone to accomplish. Changing Morgana's heart and her alliance was the tipping point in this war. We owe you a greater debt of gratitude than you may understand." She blushed fully at this.

Ishmael came forward with the pearl and diamond woven crown. The gems lay around the crown in an intricate, woven halo, crafted from the very stone the streets were made from.

Alder Spoke: "With the unfortunate and sad passing of the beautiful Queen Evana I present to you a warrior, who fought and risked his life to help end the war. A selfless individual who did everything he could for the protection of his people. I have no doubt that he will lead the elven race into a bright future, and it'll be stronger than it ever was before. Lee Odion, do you accept this coronation and the responsibilities that follow?"

Lee looked up at him and bowed. "I humbly accept and understand my responsibilities."

"By the power bestowed in me as Prince of Everworld I now pronounce you King Lee Odion of Algernon." Applause erupted from the crowd as Ishmael laid the beautiful halo crown over the head of the new king.

Lee turned to face everyone. "I promise to be fair and just. I swear to lead by example. I ask for your trust as I do my best to guide our wonderful race into the future. Thank you all and may Queen Evana's spirit and all the spirits of the kings and queens of old rest in peace."

Alder continued: "Chief Annikan was a chief unlike any other to this day. The Natarians are feared for their dedication to the protection of their lands. Annikan was the driving force of the fierce love and determination that seeps from the very pours of all Natarians. The Valley of Shadows grew with him as your leader and he will surely be missed and never forgotten. Taking his place is a young man with a lot to learn, but I ask for the patience of all Natarian people that Ahawi and elders will raise him well and train him to be a fighting warrior just like his predecessor." He bent down to look into the eyes of Tokano whose sapphire eyes shined bright in the sunlight. "Young Tokano, do you accept and understand what is happening here today? You will be crowned chief and must learn the ways to lead your people. It is a big responsibility but I believe you have what it takes under the guidance of your mother. And I know she believes you have what it takes as well. Do you accept and understand these responsibilities. This is no game, but I ask you do not be afraid and show these people now you have the courage they can trust in."

Tokano dropped to one knee emulating Lee just minutes before. "I will do what is necessary if you ask it, Prince Alder." He smiled.

"Sometimes a child's heart is the best to follow, for it shows only the way of desire and truth. Bow down, and allow the feather headdress to be placed upon you." Tokano bent as directed. Ahawi placed the crown of feathers upon his head and kissed his cheek.

"Don't you worry, I trust and believe in you, and I'll be here every step of the way."

Alder spoke again: "I present to you, by the powers bestowed in me, High Chief Tokano." Applause erupted once again at the crowning of the youngest high chief to ever walk the valley.

"Alas we come to Mallory Bones. As you are from Earth we have no coronation for you, but we do have a gift for your courage and bravery." Mallory looked confused. Crimson stepped forward from his place previously beside her. He raised his finger at the fountain where Alder stood. Alder stepped down and aside. A swirl of lightning and wind circled his finger before a bolt shot out and inscribed first an "m" and then a "b" in the middle of the fountain just below her father's same initials. She began to cry tears of joy and hugged Crimson who stood in shock being foreign to signs of affection. She let go and rushed to hug Alder who wrapped his arms around her. Tears fell from both of Morgana's eyes. Mallory came back and hugged her mother. After the trio of hugs she returned to Alder.

"What will Everworld do now?" Mallory asked.

"We will live on. We will rebuild and continue to grow as individuals and as one," he replied. Mallory smiled at this and made her way over to Lee.

"Lee, before my mother and I depart tomorrow can we take one last stroll to Koel's memorial gravesite?" She looked up hopefully at him.

"Of course, Mallory," he responded and smiled back. Festivities continued for the rest of the afternoon in celebration of a new beginning. Later that evening Mallory and Lee came upon the gravestone and memorial marked for Koel Lo'Hota.

"If you ever come back to visit us, I promise you a statue will stand here in his honor." Lee grabbed her hand and gently squeezed.

She let go of his hand and turned to hug him. "Lee," she said, "thank you for everything. You came so far with me and risked your life. I owe you mine." She propped up to the tip of her toes and kissed his cheek.

"You showed me courage beyond my wildest dreams. I'll never forget you, Mallory Bones."

"I'll never forget you, Lee Odion. King…King Lee Odion."

Hand in hand they made their way back to Algernon where everyone had begun to depart.

Mallory made her way over to Ahawi and hugged her. "Thank you Ahawi, for fighting for us."

Ahawi smiled. "Of course, Mallory Bones, child from Earth. I will always remember you. Please stay safe in your future travels." Ahawi approached Alder and whispered to him. "Where is your general, Scarlet? Shouldn't she be attending the coronations and festivities?"

Alder whispered back: "I sent her on a mission to gather intelligence about the whereabouts of Azaroth." To this, Ahawi nodded.

Mallory hugged Tokano one last time before the new king and Ahawi departed leading their fellow men and women back to the valleys.

Alder approached Mallory. "I shall spend the night here and see you off tomorrow."

"Okay," Mallory responded and smiled. She met up with Morgana as both were given beds in the now king's house for the night. Tomorrow they'd return home to fight another battle.

Chapter 27

GOING HOME

Deep inside her heart she mourns
But on the surface she glows
She represses the things she can't control
And lets her emotions go

She's haunted by faults
The dead have come back to life
The light re-enters

Sunshine broke into the room – a sunshine that would brighten up a mood to battle a sadness to follow. Mallory got dressed and made her way downstairs to where Morgana was already waiting for her with Lee. They stepped outside to see Alder waiting near the fountain for them with Ishmael. In Ishmael's hands was a book. On the black book was written nothing but the words "My Tale." On the cover sat a symbol. The symbol was a circle with an "M" the stretch of its diameter and a "T" that filled it the opposite way.

"Good morning Alder, Ishmael," Mallory said.

"Good morning," they replied.

"Are you ready to go home, Mallory Bones, and are you ready to go home Morgana Bones?" Alder asked.

They both looked at each other and responded at the same time. "Yes, we are."

Alder detached the symbol from the cover and placed it in Mallory's hands. "Hold onto that and hold on to your mother's hand tightly. The force of you leaving will also drag her along with you." He paused for a minute while staring at her.

"What is it?" Mallory questioned.

"You're destined for great things. I can sense it." Mallory smiled. "Goodbye Mallory Bones."

"Goodbye Prince Alder," she replied.

Alder flipped open the cover of the book and a blinding white light surrounded Mallory and Morgana.

Daniel closed the book and set it down. Michael's dying breaths were too hard to bear. "As far as I'm aware they should be back," he said.

"They'll be here." Each word Michael said was separated by a nasty cough. He gasped for air over and over before catching his breath.

Meanwhile, *A Darn Good Read* had reappeared on the street where Mallory's curiosity got the better of her a few weeks prior. The brightness that accompanied the switching of worlds snapped away quicker this time. Both mother and daughter looked at each other.

"Daddy!" Mallory yelled.

"Michael!" Morgana said and the two began to race toward the door of the bookstore.

"Wait!" Mallory yelled and turned around hoping to snap back to Everworld quick to ask about what to do with the symbol but when she turned around Lee Odion was standing inside the bookshop.

"So, this is Earth?" Lee asked.

Mallory smiled with joy and giggled. "Yes, but this is simply a bookstore."

Lee smiled at this and looked at her. "In your rush to see your father and in your excitement you forgot to say goodbye to me."

Mallory felt ashamed and felt her face heat up.

"I came to take the symbol back to Everworld. We don't need any more strangers appearing there."

"But, how will I get back?" she started to ask before Alder's words came back to her. She's already come to Everworld once so she won't need the emblem again. She placed it in the outstretched hand of Lee. He closed his fingers around it and looked one more time at her.

"Goodbye, Mallory Bones. I truly hope it's not forever." he said and smiled.

"It won't be. It can't be. I'll make sure of that." She smiled and they embraced in a final hug before Lee flipped open the book and disappeared into a blinding white flash. "Daddy," she whispered and grabbed her mother's hand again. The two ran out of the bookstore and all the way back to their house.

Michael and Daniel both heard a door fly open downstairs and feet fly up the narrow staircase that led to the master bedroom.

Through the doorway came a young girl with straw-colored hair and a woman all presumed to be dead. Mallory rushed to his side. Morgana sat frozen in fear but the ice was thawed when Daniel swung his arms around his baby girl and cried.

"Mallory, I'm so happy you're alive," he began.

"Daddy, I'm so sorry. I tried my best to save you. I did everything I could. I'm so sorry. I'm so sorry!" Tears began to stream down her cheeks but Michael's weak hand lifted and wiped them away. He suppressed all urges to cough.

"Don't be sad my little angel." He chocked a cough down. "You can't save everyone all the time. I have never been more proud of you. You're going to become the most beautiful woman." He brushed at her hair and looked over at Morgana.

"Michael…" Morgana's voice quivered.

"Morgana." Michael's voice was more solid.

"I'm so sorry for everything," she said. She looked over at Michael and walked to the other side of the bed and grabbed his hand. "I don't deserve anything but bitterness and resentment from you. I was a terrible human being and now you're dying and I can't save you. I'm sorry." Tears began to fall onto his bed, staining the sheets with salt. "It should be me dying, not you."

"No," he said. "Morgana, I will love you until the end of time. The mistake you made was terrible, there's no doubt about that but I'm dying. I'm too weak to hold a grudge. I forgive you if Mallory does and from what I read, she does."

"What do you mean daddy? What do you mean from what you've read?" Mallory's confused look prompted Daniel to hand the book over.

Mallory quickly scanned and flipped through the pages and slowly came to realize her entire adventure in Everworld was written inside the book. "You watched me every step of the way, didn't you?"

"I sure did sweetheart. Why do you think I'm so proud of you?"

Mallory thought rapidly before responding. "That was your voice during the riddles that I heard wasn't it? I knew it!" Mallory didn't let him answer.

"Yes," he said choking down another cough. "I can't hold on much longer. Today is my last, I'm sure of it.

"Alder, Ishmael, Annikan and Lee send their love to you," she said.

"They all know I love them too." He turned back to Morgana. "If you're truly sorry you'll take care of our little girl from now on. Bring her up right and teach her well."

"Of course, my love," she answered.

He gasped for air over and over, he caught it back. "It's time for me to say goodbye."

"Daddy! No!" Mallory began again.

"Sweetheart, it's okay. Be the strong woman I know you can be and trust you will become," he repeated. "I love you, so very much."

"I love you too, very, very much." Mallory cried.

"Morgana, I still love you. Thank you for all the wonderful years together."

"I love you too. Thank you for everything," Morgana replied, crying harder.

"Daniel?"

"Yes, my son?" Daniel responded.

"Thank you for everything you've done. Thank you for allowing me to marry your daughter and have my own. Thank you for taking care of me and them when I grew weak. I love you."

"I love you too, son." Tears began to stream down his cheeks as well. He let them fall refusing to brush them away.

"Mallory," he said with barely any breathe.

"Yes daddy?"

"Go on more adventures for me, okay?"

"I'll go on all of the adventures for you."

Michael smiled with the remainder of his strength. "No matter where you go, I'll always be with you." His hands went limp and dropped with these final words and his heart beat no longer. A final gasp escaped his lips and he passed on. His spirit would watch over them always.

Chapter 28

A NEW TALE

An adventurer never stops
They seek until there is no more to see
But there's always more to see
Always more to do and always more to be

Sunshine entered through her window as she peered out into a wild, blue sky that left her imagination wide open and running. The death of her father was the toughest thing Mallory ever faced, even after dealing with her experiences in Everworld. She opened the window to a calm breeze flowing in and warmth radiating on her skin. Summer was here and there wasn't a moment to lose. Her mother had gone to get groceries and her grandfather decided to move in to help take care of them. He was the only source of income, and he had to come up with some lunatic story of how Morgana came home a couple nights after they got back from Everworld. Luckily there was no evidence of anything so the authorities had no choice but to declare her as 'undead'. Her fingerprints matched those of her records. Nothing like this had ever happened before so they were at a loss. Her gravestone was removed and Michael's was put in its place. The funeral went as smoothly as possible and soon things began to settle down once again. Mallory became home-schooled by a private teacher and Morgana began to look for a job. Daniel's pension was paying the bills and things were moving along just fine.

Mallory decided to visit her father's grave. She wore a nice pair of lightly faded jeans and a light tee-shirt. She passed by where the bookstore that changed her life had been but it was gone. Somehow this didn't surprise her as she just smiled at the vacant location and at the memories it brought her. She arrived at his grave and placed a sunflower, her favorite, and sat and talked to him for a while, filling her dad in on everything going on at home. She finished and kissed the headstone before leaving.

On her walk back she looked over expecting a vacant lot but the bookstore was there again. She rubbed her eyes in disbelief and rushed inside.

"Hello?" she said, but no one answered. It was vacant. Every fiber of her being wanted to travel to Everworld but her heart told her not to. It just wasn't the right time. She tried not to question it and walked back to where she was first gifted the book. She remembered the face of the man with the salt and pepper hair. This made her smile too. She ran her finger along edges of the books, looking at the titles one by one. *The Lands of Forgotten Time* sat on top of the bookshelf where she had left it when the man disappeared. She re-read the back and put it away. I'll save that one for a rainy day. She giggled to herself at this joke as the sun outside heated the inside of the bookstore.

"Ugh," she said grossed out, "it's hot in here."

To the left of *The Lands of Forgotten Time* was a series of books she remembered seeing, titled *Autumn Knight*. Book number one of the series was called *Autumn Knight and the Whispering Willows*. She read the back, figured it seemed like fun so she took it with her and proceeded to leave the store. Before she reached the door she heard a voice from behind her.

"Be careful." She gasped and jumped. She turned around expecting the man but no one was there. The voice continued, "Interjecting yourself into a story is dangerous, even if you're just along for the ride. New adventures hold unknown dangers. Even the smallest changes have consequences." She thought carefully about this and pressed the book to her chest before leaving the store. The minute she turned around it was gone again.

"My life will never be normal again," she said and laughed at herself and headed home.

When she arrived her mother was back from the store with the groceries. Morgana asked what she had been up to and Mallory told her about going to Michael's grave and talking with him. She ruled out telling her about the bookstore because she believed that was just too much right now. It was still a little too soon with everything.

"What's that in your hands?" Morgana saw the book peeking out from between her arms.

"Oh! I stopped at the library and borrowed this book," Mallory lied. She had recently gotten a new library card because of her home-schooling but this book wasn't from there. Not unless libraries appeared and disappeared at will. She finished helping her mother put the groceries away and told her she was going to go upstairs and start reading it.

She entered through her bedroom door and sat down at her reading chair. Mallory looked at the clock on her wall. It read five minutes to two in the afternoon. She read the back of the book again and flipped it over to the cover which showed a picture of a young girl with raven hair heading into a thick forest of willow trees. She leaned back and made herself comfortable.

"I can't wait to see where my next adventure takes me," she said and she opened the cover into a whole new world.

www.ingramcontent.com/pod-product-compliance
Lightning Source LLC
Chambersburg PA
CBHW070351200726
48294CB00003B/845